T0196342

GAMBLE
WITH THE
SUN

PHIL FORD

authorHOUSE®

AuthorHouse™
1663 Liberty Drive
Bloomington, IN 47403
www.authorhouse.com
Phone: 1 (800) 839-8640

Published by AuthorHouse 06/28/2017

ISBN: 978-1-5246-9810-2 (sc)
ISBN: 978-1-5246-9808-9 (hc)
ISBN: 978-1-5246-9809-6 (e)

Library of Congress Control Number: 2017910110

Print information available on the last page.

CONTENTS

GAMBLE WITH THE SUN

"Turner, will you step into my office for a moment?"

The middle aged Coordinator walked just ahead of the younger Turner through the lab and between the rows of research tables. He stepped through his office door, allowed Turner to step in as well and then closed the door. Making his way behind the desk, the Coordinator sat in the modest, comfortably worn, yet warm looking leather office chair.

The two men look very similar as they sat on opposite sides of the acrylic work desk. Both had rich brown eyes that embraced a look of unswerving determination. Yet, the Coordinator's eyes carried with them a slightly disconnected glare hinting to an extra weight being carried. A look he would not allow himself to translate into words, but something he bore like an old friend, an ever present sense of distraction.

By contrast, Turner's brown eyes were vibrant and clear. When he looked at someone, he looked at them fully. So intensely, there were times when passersby would give Turner a measured double-take after being surprisingly caught by his open and attentive eyes. Turner was aware when this was happening; and at times, he even relished in the response and added an extra little smile of recognition.

The Coordinator opened the conversation. "Your request checks out Turner, and by all calculations our region is long overdue for an increase in the vitamin quality of our food supplement distribution. But, we've hit the same old wall with the Council. They just do not agree. They have chosen to ignore the data, overlook the obvious, and again have denied your request.

Exasperated, Turner began a string of questions. "Do they have any idea about what they're doing? It's been three years since our last adjustments. Can we still argue with them about this? Do we stand a chance of changing their minds?"

"I'm afraid not, Turner. Each time I enter that Council room I have such hope; a hope renewed by the results of our studies and the clear and certain declarations indicated by the data from our research." After a pause, the Coordinator continues, "I've tried and I've consistently left the Council chamber terribly dismayed." The Coordinator's voice tapered off almost to a whisper, "I have this growing dread that; that maybe it's happening again; but I…"

"What's that Sir?" Turner questioned.

"What? Oh; nothing," finished the Coordinator while making an obvious effort to change the subject. "If you're not already into a project for the day, I'd like for you to re-check the results of the radiation we released into our little experiment last quarter. I'm very curious about the long range effects that specific release might have on the fish and plant life we placed in the control tanks." And then in a faint whisper, the Coordinator continued, "I suppose it might be time…"

Turner replied, "Of course. I'll take a few samples and check the outcomes again. What was that you were saying at the end Sir?"

"Just recalling my day with the Council." With a growing smirk on his face, the Coordinator continued, "As I'm sure you know Turner, I don't handle rejection very well." He paused, then with a full smile said, "You remember the year we camped out near the old coal mines in southeastern Kentucky, don't you?"

"Sure, a trip worth reliving," responded Turner with a fresh smile starting on his own face.

"It was a painful time of true rejection for me," pouted the Coordinator with his smirk growing. "I sat on that river bank for six long hours without catching a single fish."

"Are you still going on about that?" Leaning back in his chair with a smirk of his own taking over his expression, Turner continued, "With what I caught that day, we had plenty to eat."

"All the worse," exclaimed the Coordinator, a true smile stretching across his face now. "I was not only rejected by the lake fish, but further plotted against, for some unknown reason, with you showing me up by catching far more than you could ever eat yourself."

The two of them were barely holding back their laughter as Turner said, "Pardon me Sir, but your unknown reason was all too obvious."

"It was, was it? And what would that be?"

"Sir, you sat there for six hours spouting various bits of philosophy surrounding all of the known categories in the universe. During your ongoing dissertation, the fish took your lax in pole-hook concentration and slowly nibbled away the bait from the end of you hook. For six hours, you not once pulled the line to check your hook to re-bait it."

The two of them broke into full laughter, rich with the warmth shared by true friends. It was obvious they had laughed together often before. They shared this moment naturally, with the ease of familiarity.

As the laughter wound down, Turner stood and began walking to the door. "I start now on those radiation results."

The Coordinator still held a smile, but it was being gradually replaced by a growing look of exhaustion. He nodded with affirmation and half raised a hand waving as Turner left his office.

Turner walked through the numerous lab tables set in groups throughout the lab to his own set of tables. His work area took up one whole corner of the lab with no windows to distract. Performing his duties as the Assistant Coordinator meant, in part, the coordination and performance of a high volume of experiments. The tables currently represented the activity of five ongoing experiments, one of which was the radiation testing him and his friend had just discussed.

Turner's lab tables took up a bit more space to make room for Turner to move through and around them with ease. Turner did not look the part of your average, intellect driven lab worker. His broad shouldered, athletic frame never quite fit his interest and role in the field of electro-chemical analysis. He, like the Coordinator, looked more at home on a playing field rather than being surrounded by active oscilloscopes, electromagnetic generators and gravity stimulators.

But the visual inconsistency was understandable in the light of the Council's educational selection process, which seem to begin earlier with each succeeding generation. In Turner's case, his Science aptitude scores were early indicators of where the Council felt he could best serve the

Society. By the time Turner was nine years old, his education path was decided. He still was very active in any sport he chose, and good at most of them. But his service to the Society was through his intellect and not to entertain through sporting escapades. He enjoyed his intellectual pursuits. His capability and aptitude in this arena excelled. Still, Turner was more comfortable running or swimming rather than being metaphorically connected to his lab area.

"I have a quick announcement to make that concerns all of you; if I could have your attention for a moment." The Coordinator was now standing in the center of the lab waiting to continue. "I have heard the Sun is especially bright today and I also know for a fact that this department is ahead on its current endeavors. So, in short, I am personally declaring the balance of the day as a free day. You may all clean up and leave for the day. Thanks you for your attention." With a quick half turn, the Coordinator walked past his staff, walking back to his office, and closed the door behind him.

"What do you make of that Turner?" questioned one of the other lab workers. "The Coordinator is rarely this big hearted on a regular work day."

"I'm not sure; but he's right about the sunshine and there's no way I'm going to turn that offer down. Let's pack up." Turner organized and sectioned off his area with the red draw chains that acted as polite reminders that the area was off limits and stepping past them into Turner's work area was not allowed.

Turner walked over to the Coordinator's door to let him know everyone had taken his advice and were gone. He knocked on the Coordinator's door a couple of times with no response, then turned and walked away speaking to himself, "I don't blame him. A rest break and some sleep will be good medicine for him. He has clearly outworked all of us these past few weeks."

Turner left the lab, walked through the sanitary looking halls of the science building, and took the airlift down to the worker's locker room. There, he went to his locker and exchanged his lab clothing for a change of clothing consisting of a gray tee shirt, running shorts and comfortable running shoes.

In the city, since no automated land vehicles were allowed for normal inner-city transportation with the exception of a few electric delivery vehicles and limited mass-trans carriers, people were mostly on foot.

Some chose bicycles, but most walked the paths between city locations. For Turner, he chose to make the best of it embracing these travel time opportunities for one of his favorite exercises and pass times by running nearly everywhere.

Dressed for success, Turner left the science building and headed toward the southern portion of the city. He ran smoothly along the building lanes passing many of the city's residents who had chosen to walk. His breathing started harsh and heavy as always; but when he hit his stride and found that point when his lungs were comfortably acclimated to the outside air and his muscles were in a rhythm of easy exhilaration, the combination brought a smile to his face. He thought at times it made him look like he had just gotten the punch line to a joke long after the joke was shared, and his expression drew some looks for those he passed. That was the plateau he sought. When he reached this level, Turner felt he could run forever. In his zone, Turner had been running for about thirty minutes. He was not trying to beat any speed records or push himself to any new level of muscle stress to increase his strength. He just flowed through the city landscape as if he were flowing across a liquid surface.

It was at this point in today's jaunt that Turner recognized a friend along the path ahead of him. This was unusual for Turner to see a friend this early in the day. Being set free, so to speak, so early in the day appeared to have its advantages. It was also unusual for him to run across a friend since he had only a few close friends. Turner was very sociable. He had numerous acquaintances whom he shared pleasant times with, but very few true friends. Turner coined a phrase for this seeming dichotomy he lived; to be associated with so many people whom he enjoyed spending brief amounts of time with, but not needing or really desiring to spend any time with more than one or two specific individuals. He called himself a Social Hermit. Comfortable enough within himself to be happily solitary, but not disliking the association he might have with many others for brief periods throughout the day.

Sara was a close friend. Maybe his closest. The Coordinator was a close friend as well. But there was a chemistry so natural between he and Sara, it seemed to have been in place even before they met. It was Sara that Turner saw running along the same path just ahead. "Sara, wait up."

"Turner, hi! You're out awfully early, aren't you?" She slowed her pace.

As Turner caught up to Sara he said, "I know. The Coordinator decided today would be a better day if it were a free day. So, he turned us loose. To add to that, he's been in a peculiar mood lately. I think he's exhausted himself these past few weeks and is probably catching up on some much needed sleep as we speak. Where you headed?"

"Nowhere in particular, "Sara answered, both still keeping a gradual stride of motion. "I was just running to get outside. The sky is so clear today I couldn't bear staying at my apartment."

The two of them continued to run along the lanes. Not talking much. Saving their wind for their run. They seemed to fit quite well together as they sharply cut corners while shooting past others along the lanes. Their pace was methodically matched.

Sara's long brown hair hung loosely around her shoulders and was blown back just beyond her neck by the wind as they ran. It had a way of accenting her attractive poise. Her beautiful blue eyes gained a special glitter in the blazing sunlight as they vibrantly guided her, almost willing her to go faster to embrace all should could possibly encounter.

Turner made an offer, "Let's head down to the lake for a swim. Sound good?"

Sara smiled and replied, "Great! Last one there has to clean both apartments."

Turner didn't wait to reply, but ran on ahead to get a surprise head start.

The city's lake could only loosely be described as a lake. Its geographic size was more that of an inland sea, but its depth was rarely more than 200 feet. One of the city's primary features, the lake was a drawing and gather point for many. With the lake was still about a half a mile away. Their run did not break into a sprint, but their pace did quicken. Switching back and forth between leading at one point, to following at the next, both Sara and Turner moved across the path with the ease of familiarity. Their footfalls were comfortably placed with a blend of determination and enjoyment in each new stride.

As they completed the last turn coming close to making contact with the lake's tackle and small boat storage building, Sara took the path on the inside cutting in front of Turner allowing the view of the lake to come into her view first. What she saw caused her to stutter-step bringing Turner very close to colliding into her.

"Turner, look!"

"Whoa," reaching out to Sara's shoulders and bracing the two of them preventing an outright collision as they suddenly slowed to a stop. "I see what you mean. Let's get closer." Turner looked to their right, down the low profile, decorative fence line that separated the lake from the surrounding pedestrian path. "Follow me."

With that, the two of them resumed running, but at a much slower pace now. Sara followed Turner about ten feet behind and noticed where he was headed. There was a slightly lower spot in the fence line where the natural cedar lattice was only about three feet high. As they arrived at the low spot, neither slowed but gracefully hurdled the fence coming to a halt as their feet hit the large lake's rich brown, sandy beach.

"Their dead Turner; hundreds of them." Sara's voice trailed off in shock as they took in the sight. In numbers too high to count, in an area around the lake normally covered with relaxing or frolicking groups of people, the beach was instead covered, nearly layered, with dead and dying fish. Fish of all types and sizes covered the beach all along the water's curve that created this oft times oasis of peace. "What could have caused this?"

With puzzlement in his voice, Turner responded, "Some type of pollution I suppose. But there's been no mention of any contamination for years."

Slowly, Sara and Turner began moving closer to the gruesome sight. The guards may have been there all along and gone unnoticed by the two of them having their attention drawn so completely to the fish, but seemingly out of nowhere three Council Guards came abruptly between them and the beach.

"This beach is closed. You two need to move on; leave, now," forcefully spoke the guard in the middle.

"Oh, it's alright. I'm a chemical analyst. I need to get closer to begin researching the cause of this apparent contamination."

The middle guard continued, "We have clear orders to only allow Class A analysts near the lake. The two of you Class A?"

"No, but..." Turner was quickly interrupted.

"Then move on," barked the guard. "Clear the area, now. We have our orders and they will be enforced by any method necessary."

Puzzled, but certain of the guard's resolve, Turner and Sara turned their backs towards the lake and began heading to the gated break in the fence. Both held looks of deep consideration across their faces as they silently made their way to their apartment complex, still shocked by the guard's forceful attitude at their apparent intrusion on the beach.

As they walked through the entrance door of their apartment building and towards the airlift, Sara spoke. "Have you ever seen the Council Guards anywhere near that close to force?"

"No," quietly responded Turner. "I guess it's possible they wanted to avoid the possible panic that could surround a contamination of that magnitude. But still, they were on the edge of violence and confident they were within their scope." Turner paused, head aiming at the floor, but looking nowhere. "My Coordinator will no doubt be called in to study this one." The thought seemed to give Turner a handle on the situation. "Tomorrow I'll check with him and see if I can get some answers."

CHAPTER 2

The next morning found Turner busy at his work station. With the event at the lake the evening before, he wanted to get an earlier than normal start. Finding the Coordinator was not in his office yet, Turner began working at his station and had nearly finished with his first scheduled assignment.

A co-worker stepped up to Turner with a solemn look on his face. "Turner, have you heard?" Turner thought it may have something to do with the lake's fish kill, but kept that to himself.

"Heard what Smith?"

"Our boss, the Coordinator, killed himself yesterday. They say it happened shortly after he let us go. What a shock, you know?" Smith paused, then said, "Oh, and the Commander wants to see you immediately."

"No, I hadn't heard." Turner was in shock, pure shock. He had worked for the Coordinator for ten years, ever since graduating for the University. They were friends as well. Turner knew his friend seemed taxed both mentally and physically over the past month, but he would never have expected this man to break under the pressure of anything Turner could imagine.

"Smith, watch my tables for me for a few minutes. I'm going to find out what the Commander wants."

Turner did not pause to remove his lab coat. He walked directly out to the lobby, to the airlift, and rode it to the 75th floor where the offices of the Commander were located. While on the airlift, his mind drifted to the scores of happy times he and the Commander had shared. The two were very close, at least most of the time. There seemed to be a recurring separation perpetuated by the Coordinator at unexpected times. It was something that troubled Turner a bit, but never enough to cause him to invade the privacy his friend was silently seeking.

"Can I help you?"

Turner's reverie was interrupted by the inquisitive lady at the reception counter now visible from the opened airlift doors. He spoke as if fighting through a thick fog in his brain, "Yes. I'm Turner E-6. My Coordinator died yesterday. I was told the Commander wished to speak with me."

With a subdued smile, the lady said, "Let me check for you."

Turner stood in place as the receptionist stepped through the Commander's office doorway, returning moments later saying, "Yes Turner; he'll see you now. Please follow me."

After Turner entered the Commander's office, the receptionist closed the door behind him. Turner found the Commander standing and stepping from behind his large acrylic desk. The Commander was an overweight man whose height was somewhat less than Turner's. The Commander extended his hand to Turner and they shook hands. Turner immediately noticed the limp handshake. Turner came to a quick judgement that the Commander was a man unfamiliar with physical labor or exercise. From the Commander's slouchy stance, Turner felt his assumption could not be too far off.

But the most troubling message Turner received from this jelly fish handshake was an unspoken signal of a lack of commitment to the moment. Turner could feel immediately that the death of the Coordinator, his friend, meant nothing to his superior.

"This won't take long Turner. I understand you worked with your Coordinator for some time; was it none or ten years? No matter, I'm sure based on your work experience you can understand the complexity of the position. I want you to fill the open position, effective immediately. All of the usual promotion benefits are bestowed of course." The Commander had slowly made his way to his high-backed, leather office chair and made himself comfortable while making this vague offer of support. "I'm always here if you have a problem."

"If I am your choice for the position, I will fill it." Turner's voice was solemn. The shock of his friend's death had hardly sunk in and the coldness of the Commander's push-forwardness left a sick feeling deep within Turner's stomach. "Is there anything else?"

"No Turner." The Commander stood and offered his hand to Turner across the large desk. "Welcome to management Turner."

Turner stood and turned from the Commander's outstretched hand without a flinch. He felt if he did not retreat from the presence of this buffoon, his disgust would release itself without restraint. The Commander did not appear bothered by the gesture in the slightest.

Turner's fists were clinched as he entered the airlift and made his way back to the lab. He slowly walked into the Coordinator's office that has so quickly become his own. He stopped in the doorway as he noticed a woman gently packing the personal items the Coordinator had neatly displayed around the office.

She spoke slowly and softly, "I hope you don't mind. I'm not moving very quickly. I'm still a bit shaken by his leaving."

Turner wanted to reply with some words of comfort and kindness, but he was at a loss. The picture of the middle-aged lady caressing each item before she placed it into the packing-paper filled boxes pierced his chest causing him to make an effort to choke back tears.

She stood near her husband's desk, lightly, yet controllably, crying with a small, lone, delicate tear trickling down her cheek. Her once dark brown hair was broken up with streaks of gray, all of which was tucked up and under a plain, but perfectly fitting simple, black hat.

It was as if her self-assurance was being packed into the boxes with each object once belonging to her life-long companion. It was evident to Turner theirs must have been a loving marriage. One built on more than love and the acceptance of each other, but also intertwined with a caring, sincere friendship, which had just now received a sudden and unexpected blow of bewilderment.

Turner offered, "If you'd rather be alone…?"

"No. You're Turner, aren't you?" She spoke quietly.

Turner responded, "Yes. Have we met?"

"No. Your Coordinator, my husband, mentioned you often. He described you in such careful detail I feel I already know you. You see, Turner, my husband and I never had any children of our own. He never really opened up to me about all of his reasons, but he would say this world was in too much of a mess to force another human being to be brought into it. I suppose that's why he's seemed to pay so much attention to you, Turner. He really thought of you as his son."

She continued, "He even left a message for you. It sounds like an incomplete request; but, he told me just the day before his dying if he should die, I must give you this message. He said you should pursue the radiation results of the Aquarian project. That's it – nothing more. I hope it means something to you."

Turner tried offering his condolences and felt his words empty, but heartfelt. He left her to her packing offering to help with anything she may need.

Returning to his work tables, Turner thought it over but did not see any clear meaning behind the Coordinator's message. The tests were over two years old. They did not appear to have any current value except the Coordinator had said something about the Council being interested in reviewing the results. With this and the new message in mind, Turner walked to the communications screen and called the Commander's receptionist.

"Yes Turner?" spoke the Commander.

"I wanted to assure you I would continue re-checking the results of the Aquarian project for the Council as you requested."

"Turner, excuse me, but I believe today has been too much for you. Neither the Council nor I have any need for a recap on a two-year-old project, especially that one. Maybe you should take the balance of the day off and get some rest. Now, if you will excuse me, this Division must go on."

The screen went black. Turner sat there bewildered. Not by the Commander's lack of compassion; Turner had seen that before. He was bewildered by the Commander's response to the mention of a project important enough to the Coordinator that it was the last message he passed on to Turner. Too many unconnected thoughts at this point. Turner decided to take up on the Commander's offer and leave for the day.

After changing in the staff locker room, Turner wasted no time and went straight to Sara's apartment. The run he employed was not one of relaxation, but rather one of determination.

Sara answered the door and welcomed him in with surprise at the timing of his visit; but seeing his expression, asked no questions. She ventured into her kitchen and started steeping a cup of Turner's favorite hot tea, Earl Grey. The tea poured and ready, Sara found Turner sitting in her living room, but not comfortably. Turner was instead sitting on the front edge of her wing-backed side chair. Usually he would lounge on her sofa, but not this time.

He accepted the tea, thanked her, and took a careful sip. Whether it was the gesture or the timing, Turner began to open up. Sara saw that he was clearly confused. She sat silently sipping her own tea and listened. He paused several times; contemplated; sipped tea, and would continue. This went on for a few minutes until Turner seemed to come to a conclusion.

"Sara, the Coordinator's message means something. I know it does. But I can't take the chance in continuing any experiments at the science building's lab. The response the Commander gave me when I mentioned the project says to me it's a hot item. It felt like the Commander would probably exile me from the Colony if I were found doing that research."

Turner hesitated for a moment, and then continued, "What if we were to work on the project in my lab in the apartment? It would afford us privacy. What about it Sara?"

Without hesitation, Sara looked straight into Turner's eyes and said, "Sure. If you feel strongly about it, we'll do the complete research project if necessary until you're confident with the results."

The dawn had become imminent as the blazing Sun sifted its colors of orange and yellow through the gracefully puffed clouds barely hanging above the horizon. As Turner ran, an abundance of prismed reflections projected multicolored rays against a backdrop of concentrated metallic structures scored along the walkways of the Colony's capital from their solar-angle panels atop each of the myriad-leveled complexes.

Turner ran towards the doorway of the complex. He came to the doorway and spoke into the voice control, "Entrance sequence, Turner E-6." The air locked doors slid apart into the sidewalls allowing Turner to enter. After his entrance, the door swiftly closed behind him. Unlike the fifteen levels above the ground, Turner's apartment was on the sixth sub-level below the structure. Turner boarded the air lift and again parroted, "Entrance sequence, Turner E-6."

It had been four months since the Coordinator's death. Turner and Sara had continued with their at-home experiments. "At least I still have my own research lab," Turner thought to himself. I can't imagine only performing my mechanical functions for the Council."

During the third month after the Coordinator's death, Turner had been contacted by a private retirement firm in reference to his former Coordinator's Last Will and Testament. The Coordinator had made arrangements for accounts for his wife, but he had also set up investments jointly owned by the Coordinator and Turner, about which Turner was never aware.

In his Will, the Coordinator had left instructions for the retirement firm, upon his death, to convert all of the joint investments to cash and place them in a private, secured account solely in Turner's name. It had taken the three months to liquidate the sizable investments in a manner as to not draw undue attention to the transactions, as per the Coordinator's explicate instructions.

It had been a month now since Turner discovered the Coordinator had made Turner a multimillionaire.

Entering the room, Turner waited until the door relocked, and then walked to the dining room area where he took a small bottle down from one of the cabinets. His own creation, these pills contained the nourishment required for one complete day. The Council, if they knew, would ban any nourishment of this type – especially one not distributed by the Council itself. Turner's theory was anything he could development within his own lab would better isolate him from the compulsion of the Council to conform to their standards and procedures. Even his entry door was unique. The only other system of its type was located down the hallway from Turner on the door of its inventor, Sara.

Sitting on the comfortable, well-worn, over-sized cushion chair, Turner studied some of the notes made from his experiments to recheck the results of the Aquarian Project. Silently he pondered page after page paying close attention to the sequential progress of the equations and their explanations.

Behind Turner was the rarely used video screen. Stretching six feet square with a slightly concave curvature, it was the primary tool used by the Council to spread the high volume of propaganda deemed necessary to keep peace in the colonies. To Turner's right and down the hallway was his private laboratory. It was quite illegal to have such a set-up at one's own disposal, which was the reason Turner disconnected the voice actuated door mechanism from the entry door.

As Turner arose and started towards the lab, the visitor signal sounded at the entry door. Turner walked to the video screen and activated it by pressing a switch on the panel to the left of the screen. The projection enlarged to a clear picture of the hallway. Standing alone outside the entry door was a woman quite familiar to Turner. It was Sara; the tall and very attractive brunette with her luminously bright eyes.

Turner, without hesitation, walked to the entry door and released the lock. The door smoothly slide open and Sara stepped in.

"It's good to see you, Sara," spoke Turner as they embraced.

"These days seem to be growing longer, Turner, with each new assignment."

"I know what you're saying, Sara. Our section just completed a new food substitute for the Eastern Quarter colonies. All we did was change the color and shape. The Council denied our request to change its composition even to increase the vitamin quality. Their reason was a shortage of vitamins supplements in the Southern Quarter."

"Sounds logical," added Sara. "The Southern Quarter has a history of high vitamin intake."

"But it can't be true, Sara. Do you remember Michael S-6 from the university?"

"Yes, he went to the Southern Quarter, didn't he?"

"He did Sara. For the last year and a half I've conferred with him on several situations. The last time we spoke I asked if he could explain why the vitamin intake had been higher in the Southern Quarter than elsewhere in the Society for the past three years," continued Turner.

"What did he say?" asked Sara.

"He was confused at my question."

"Confused! Why?" Sara asked with amazement.

"Because Michael was informed his request for a higher vitamin compliment for his Quarter would have to be indefinitely postponed due to the overly high intake here in the Eastern Quarter."

"What!? Our intake is low, almost too low!" replied Sara in a tone of raging disbelief.

"That's what I mean," said Turner in an exasperated tone.

After a few minutes of silence, Sara began, "Rather than picking up where we left off last night, let's back up three signs in the equation and start from there."

Now looking at the slate board covered with their equations, Turner replied, "Fine. Let's assume this cosine is correct. That would make 44.6 its derivative and its square root would be .022421524."

"That agrees with logic," continued Sara, "and that factor divided by pi equals -.7140612. All three factors agree with what we calculated last night. Turner, what if our calculations are correct and this equation is true?"

"Can you safely simulate the calculated effect here in the lab Sara?"

"Yes, but I'll need to modify the laser emissions unit somewhat. It won't be difficult, but it will take the rest of the evening," concluded Sara.

"Good," said Turner. "I'm going to use the time to visit the archives. Maybe there will be an answer on the old math and nuclear microfilms that will disprove our findings… I hope so."

Turner took a blank notebook and left for the Archives. The Archives' building was off limits to the main population of the Colony. Turner, though, was a Class B engineer giving him access to nearly all of the divisions of the Archives.

Upon arriving at the Archives division of Math and Nuclear Science, Turner sat immediately at the Video reading screens. He thought, "Where should I start? I think the ten years prior to the birth of the Society would be the best place to start."

He set the screen's reference selector to the year 2020 A.D., ten years before the world government collapsed and the Society emerged. The screen enabled Turner to read the conclusions of all the Math and Nuclear experiments. Within a span of two hours, Turner was able to read all of the conclusion materials from 2020 through 2029.

"Nothing unusual here," whispered Turner to himself. He read of the period of time when the nuclear plants were fully active. The governments of the world allowed full escalation of the nuclear power program to attempt to supply all of the world's electricity by 2040. The main problem, which was the specific reason for the delay in escalation prior to 2020, was the enormous amounts of nuclear waste created as a byproduct of the energy produced. This problem was, in 2020, alleviated by a process developed by the world's leading space exploration association.

The process was to load all of the nuclear waste onto inexpensively constructed cargo transports and send those transports towards the Sun where they would be destroyed by the Sun's intense heat. These transports were sent periodically as the amount of fission waste accumulated. The process seemed infallible.

"I think I'll read the material recorded from the year 2030. Maybe there's something during the Council's emergence years that will offer some enlightenment."

After an hour in front of the 2030 material, Turner's face took on a look of surprise and confusion. "These records can't be complete. The last entries before the Council's takeover have been erased from the film. It jumps from some slight anomaly noted in the nuclear transport program directly to the Council's ousting of the world' political governments."

"Excuse me," interrupted one of the Archive workers. "You have a communication at the reference station."

Turner replied, "Thank you," and walked to the station where the communication was being received. "Yes?"

"Turner, it's Sara. I completed the modifications an hour ago and have begun setting up the experiment. I'll be finished with the set-up in about a half an hour. We'll then be able to start the experiment this evening if you'll be ready?"

"I'll be there in an hour then. I just have a few more references to check before leaving."

"I'll see you then," said Sara ending the communication.

Turner returned to the video screen and set the reference selector to the year 2031. The screen shifted and then went totally blank. He attempted to reactivate the screen and the reaction was the same – totally blank.

"Excuse me," Turner said to one of the Archive workers. "Why is this screen deactivating on the 2031 setting?"

"You're Turner E-6, correct?" asked the worker.

"Yes, I am," replied Turner.

The worker continued, "That explains the deactivation then. You're of Class B clearance and the 2031 through 2040 materials require a Class A clearance."

"Class A clearance? Why?" questioned Turner.

"I don't know. I'm only Class B myself," he replied and then turned to walk away.

"Wait!" said Turner in a loud and demanding voice.

"Sir, you must be quiet. It is the norm, remember?" said the worker.

"Excuse me, you're right," said Turner. "Is there an Archive worker here with a Class A clearance that I might ask a few questions?"

"No," replied the worker. "We have no Class A workers on our staff. The only Class A representative of the Archive is the Archive Council member himself. I'm sorry I can't help you. We close in ten minutes."

"Yes," said Turner. "Thank you. I'm ready to leave." As Turner raised from his seat to leave, he began thinking of whom he might know that held a Class A clearance. He and Sara had been at the top of their fields for some time and neither had ever been approached with the possibility of a Class certification promotion to the level A.

After leaving the Archives, Turner wandered aimlessly around the Archive grounds, trying to think of a reason for such a blatant classification of records to a secret level to which only the Council members would have access. After an hour, Turner remembered he was to meet Sara and headed to the complex.

As Turner entered his apartment, he found Sara in the front room sitting lifeless on the liquid lounge with an expression totally unlike her normal look of confidence. Sara appeared lost.

"What is it Sara?" Did something go wrong? Are you alright?"

"The experiment was a success," began Sara. "If you call certain doom a success. The set-up proved our equations true. If they're as accurate as they appear, we have exactly seven months before the Earth's atmospheric protection will be charred to such a point by the radioactive Solar Winds it will diminish to almost nothing and allow the atmospheric pressure to explode from the surface of the Earth. The fish dying in the lake and the sketchy results from the Aquarian Project were only mild introductions of the effects of the radiation storm to come and of our certain doom."

"Oh my God! I prayed we were wrong. You're sure, beyond any doubt?"

"Face it, Turner, we're as good as dead!" blasted Sara as she threw her glass across the room and dropped her head into her hands crying.

"Sara," began Turner, "there must be something we can do… Warn the Council; yes, that's it. Warn the Council of our findings." Turner sighed, "I suppose that's futile at this point."

Turner sat next to Sara on the liquid lounge. He felt he knew now what reason was so devastating to his former Coordinator.

The next morning Sara awoke reaching for Turner and was startled to find him gone from the liquid lounge where they had fallen asleep in each other's arms. "Turner, are you still here?"

"I'm here," replied Turner. "I've been awake for a couple of hours. I wanted to finish our preliminary report for the Council."

"You what!? Turner, what good…"

"Sara," Turner interrupted, "we still have a responsibility to the rest of our people and the rest of the Earth, and I know it's fruitless, but what else can we do?"

"I suppose you're right," Sara sighed. "When should we give them our report?"

"Tomorrow morning," Turner replied. "I've already made the appointment."

"How did you set a hearing so quickly?" questioned Sara with a puzzled look. "It usually takes weeks to be granted time before the Council."

Turner replied, "I told them I had knowledge of a plot to execute one of the members of the Council and haste in warning them could save their life."

"Will they ever be surprised," said Sara with a smirk. "Let me clean up and I'll meet you in thirty minutes."

While Turner waited, he recalled his puzzlement in finding the incomplete Archive records. "There must be someone well versed in history we could seek out. Of course, Professor Solomon! He, of all people, should know something of that time period. When I studied under him at the Academy, he had referenced the nuclear waste removal processes often for their success."

Sara returned from her apartment and Turner relayed his puzzlement concerning the missing records. "We must contact Professor Solomon today, if possible, before the Council meeting. I'll call his complex."

Turner activated the audio-phone. "Professor Solomon? This is Turner E-6. I studied under you at the Science Academy. A matter of grave importance has arisen and I must talk with you immediately. Yes, I can be there in ten minutes. Thank you Professor."

Both Turner and Sara left to meet Professor Solomon at his complex. Passing through the street with haste, they arrived there with little delay,

Turner touched the intercom unit. "Professor Solomon, it's Turner E-6 and my friend, Sara E-6. We spoke a few minutes ago."

"Yes," replied the Professor.

The doors slid apart. Turner and Sara briskly entered after which the doors silently closed. They were me at the end of the hallway by a short, slightly overweight, gray-haired man Turner recognized as the professor.

"You sounded extremely excited, young man. I hope I can justify your excitement by making your visit worthwhile," said the professor.

Turner replied, "We hope so too Professor. We must ask you of the radioactive waste removals of the years 2020 through 2030. I searched the Archives' film banks and was informed these records are classified Class A records which is confounding especially in light of the fact even a scholar such as you has only a class B clearance."

"I'm sure there is some specific reason the two of you found interest in that period of time and those particular programs. Surely the Council has not assigned you to study those, and personal study would not benefit you in the eyes of the Council."

"Our concern," answered Sara, "is well founded and our actions in the eyes of the Council are miniscule compared to our calculated discoveries. We must know of that period of time. Can you help us?"

"I'm very apprehensive of your goal for this information," continued the professor. "But, it seems I must share my knowledge in order to learn why it could be so important to the two of you. As I remember, the waste removal program from the years of 2020 and 2029 was seemingly a work of genius by the space exploration association, as you well know from our studies in class. Then in the year 2030, a group of protestors began a series of attacks on the prevailing world governments to stop this particular method of nuclear waste removal because of an undisclosed reason."

"Undisclosed reason?" questioned Turner. "What was it?"

"I'm not sure," replied the professor. "It was never discussed or recorded in any of the available records I've read in my years of study; but, I did have a very old professor when I myself attended the Academy who came to class on his last day before his death, expressing great distress on the subject and excitedly spouting nonsense about solar winds."

"What about solar winds," questioned Sara?

"I don't know," continued the professor. "The instructor had a history of heart trouble and had a heart attack just following the close of class. I suppose it was due to his age and the great amount of stress he appeared to be under. It was a great shock to me. I thought a lot of that professor... Where was I? Oh, after his death, the subject of the protest or those undisclosed reasons never came up again. The Council took control of the world governments in 2030, and soon after ordered the complete conversion to solar energy from the previously total dependence on nuclear energy. I'm sorry, I have grown fatigued from our conversation. If you won't be offended, I'll ask you to excuse me for today so I may rest."

"Of course, Professor," replied Turner. "Thank you for your help."

"I can't see I was much help; but, if you think so, I'm glad."

"Thank you again Professor," Sara added.

The next day, following the end of the Council meeting and he and Sara returning to their apartments, Turner stood at the bar in his apartment slowly mixing two drinks. The Council had shown no interest in their results. The stupor caused by their findings had not worn off.

"I called our Commander just after we returned and told him we would not be in for a few days. He said our assignments could wait and to take all the time we want."

"Thank you Turner," Sara said softly. "I'm sure I couldn't handle just sitting there, working and knowing all we know."

Turner slowly walked from the bar over to where Sara was sitting and sat next to her on the liquid lounge. "Here's your drink, Sara."

"Thanks. It's been a long time since I started drinking before noon. Of course, I've never felt so defeated before either... You know, Turner, we've known each other for over ten tears now and in all that time I can't remember us talking about love. Our affection for each other has been obvious for years, but I've never told you I love you. I suppose since the Council's norms are against marriage, I've tried to hold back my feelings of wanting to live with you and become your wife."

"Sara, I love you too; but, why talk about love now? There's not enough time in our lives to enjoy love."

"Turner, we have seven months! Let's not waste them by working for the Council. Let's just pack up some things and leave."

21

Turner nodded his head and sat on the front edge of the liquid lounge next to Sara. He leaned back on the lounge, put his arm around Sara's shoulders, and sat staring at the ceiling.

"That's our only hope Sara – to escape," Turner spoke softly.

"What?"

"I know it sounds strange, and I have no idea how we'll do it; but, it's our only chance for survival. If we are going to live longer than the next seven months, we're going to have to escape from the Earth completely."

"What you are saying Turner is practically impossible."

Turner continued, "I know; but you'll have to admit, there is a slim possibility we could make it happen and that's more of a chance than of we accept the alternative and do nothing."

"You're right Turner. At least this way we have some hope, I guess. But what?"

"I don't know, Sara."

The two of them sat for a while, still leaning back on the lounge, gazing at the ceiling while they talked.

"Turner, if we did come up with an idea of how to leave, where would we possibly go?"

"I don't know Sara. I would imagine the trip would be a Utopia all in itself because you will be with me."

"Oh Turner," sighed Sara. "I'm sur that it would be Utopia for the both of us." She turned and lightly kissed Turner on the lips and then laid her head on his shoulder. "It would have been so awful to have discovered this disaster by myself. That would have made me so totally alone. I might have died from the anxiety."

A romantic silence settled over both Turner and Sara as they thought about their love and friendship. Never before had either one of them been face to face with death. It brought feelings and words they had always been afraid to express.

The Society's norms were very clear. Love and marriage were to be preserved for the later, less productive years of life. The Council enforced the idea until a person reached middle age, he or she owed it to the rest of the Society to give their undivided attention and energies to making their world a better place to live. Love and marriage were considered very selfish ideals that could only benefit the Society after an individual reached the age when they had gained enough knowledge and experience to pass on to their children, not when they were still learning themselves.

The Council was not against the idea of marriage; but, it was against any arrangement that lessoned the attention towards the Council objectives of those younger than middle age. So, the two of them practiced restraint in discussing marriage for fear of being ostracized.

It was nearly evening as Turner and Sara still rested on the liquid lounge, finding themselves nearly intoxicated after drinking all afternoon. The unnatural quietness was a true sign of their shock. Wasting an entire afternoon sitting around drinking would have been unimaginable during their worst moods of depression – this went far beyond any depressing thoughts they had felt before.

"Turner, when was the last time we walked in the moonlight and just gazed at the stars?"

"I can't remember the last time."

"Well, now's our chance," said Sara with an almost child-like excitement. "It's dark enough – let's go."

"You've got a date, milady. It's off to the stars!" Turner replied in a youthful manner.

The two of them stood and started toward the door in an almost skipping frolic. In no time, they were outside their complex and skipping hand-in-hand towards a small preserve of the only park for miles around. The preserve was only five blocks from their complex. The center piece of this small preserve was an ancient Oak tree. As they reached the entrance to the fenced-in area, they stopped at the preserve's edge staring at the giant Oak tree located in the center of the park area. It stood easily a hundred feet tall and was greater than a six feet across. The giant Oak's leaves covered the sky like an inviting blanket of green.

"Oh, Turner," sobbed Sara, "we just wouldn't be happy until we destroyed every living thing on what used to be a beautiful planet."

The two of them slowly walked towards the Oak tree not taking their eyes away from its visage.

"It's beautiful Sara, just beautiful."

Turner reached out with both hands and caressed the bark of the Oak and continued, "Sara, I hope I'm drunk."

"Why?"

"Because I feel like crying; that has never happened to me before; I feel so embarrassed."

"Turner," whispered Sara as she touched the back of his hand still resting on the tree, "don't be embarrassed because you feel. The norm is not important anymore. Let's just sit here by the tree, okay?"

Silently, the two of them sat down with their backs against the furrowed bark of the tree. A shivering tear slowly ran down Turner's face as he spoke, "What have we done? I mean, was progress so important we discounted the pitfalls? How could we have overlooked a reaction of this magnitude?! I cannot believe this is actually happening. I go to my assignment one morning only to find my closest friend has killed himself apparently because he knew of this, or at least suspected it since he left the message to follow up on a dated research project. I suppose his answer was a natural one. Escape completely from what will happen in a few short months. Why not?"

"Turner!" begged Sara, "don't leave me, especially by killing yourself." Sara began to openly cry as she buried her head into Turner's chest.

"I'm not thinking of leaving you Sara. This is becoming too much to handle. For the first time I can understand what my Coordinator was going through, and why he chose to leave."

It was late in the evening before Turner and Sara left the preserve for home. They both had sunken deeply into a depressed state. They hardly spoke to one another. When they arrived home, being so intoxicated, they very soon fell asleep.

Sara was a bit groggy when she awoke to the pleasant smell of fresh coffee.

"Good morning sleepy head." Turner was sitting on the side if the bed with two cups of coffee. "Time to get up and get moving. We have an appointment with the Council at 11 this morning."

"What are you talking about? Why? Is that coffee for me?"

Turner handed her the steaming coffee. "At 11 we go before the Council and tell them we want to take the rest of the time we have off from our work. They know we have discovered what's going to happen and I can't imagine them giving us any argument. Why work during this time? We wouldn't be any good at it anyway; we know too much."

"Good point. Then what do we do?"

"Well, I got up this morning feeling about the same as last night. I was moping around the apartment and remembered I had not gone through the personal papers the Commander said the Coordinator had left for me. I found quite a surprise. There was an investment summary with contact information. The coordinator bequeathed 90% of his holdings to me. I never knew he invested in the stock market at all, but wow; he made a ton on his investments. It looks like he never made a bad investment.

I called the portfolio manager who said the investments were still growing at such a rate he couldn't say for sure what the totals were, but it exceeded 1.5 billion dollars as of yesterday's market close."

Sara sat up in the bed, took the coffee, took a contemplative sip and then said, "We could go away and vacation the time we have left."

"That was part of my thinking," continued Turner. "I started thinking we could go away, but different from what you're describing. Why not try to go away from Earth? You know, go into space in search of a new home. I mean, what do we have to lose?"

Sara stopped sipping and stared at Turner. "You're serious aren't you? How could we do that? I mean really, how could we do that?"

Turner began sharing the skeleton plan he had concocted that morning and Sara's disbelief slowly transferred from surprise to disbelief to showing a hint that it was possible. "It could work, just maybe. And, seriously, if it failed, at least we would be trying to survive and not just sitting back and accepting the fate of the Earth as our own." She paused and they were both silent. Then she added, "We would need to be as secretive as possible."

"My thoughts as well. Let's meet with the Council today for our permanent leave of absence but make no mention of this." Turner continued, "It's our secret. We can start working on the details as soon as we finish with the Council meeting."

Later in the day, while walking from the Council chambers, Sara said, "Well, they had no argument about granting us a permanent leave of absence. And if you think you caught the Council off guard with your other request, you really caught me off guard."

Turner's voice was tinged with embarrassment and what sounded like a bit of fear. "I just thought, well, I ah, oh, Sara!"

Sara cracked a small smile, "What's the problem?"

Turner replied, "I'm having the hardest time trying to say what I'm thinking. The truth of the matter is you and I are going to be alone for who knows how long if we can succeed in leaving the Earth and we may be alone when we land on our new home. I felt it would be best to start out right and be married."

"So you asked the Council for permission to marry me before you asked me?" Sara was holding back her laughter at the uncomfortable position Turner had found himself in.

Turner said, "I guess I did. Sara, you remember what I told the Council? I want to spend all the time that's left with you because I love you; and, well, that's the real reason." Turner stopped and faced Sara. He took both of her hands in his. "Sara, I do want to marry you. I love you and I want to be married to you for whatever our future holds."

Sara allowed herself to stop holding back her smile. "Turner, you don't have to say any more. I love you Turner. I would love to marry you."

The next day, Turner entered the large exhibition gallery of the NASA Museum and found himself standing directly in front of the huge, almost florescent white space shuttle. He stood frozen at first in the doorway as he studied the shuttle from nose to tail. Finally, he entered and walked slowly to the rear of the ship. The wingspan was overwhelming, far wider than the doorways, and the height as it rested in the specially designed area of the museum was accommodated by extra high ceilings.

Turner was gazing at the shuttle with such concentration that he drew the attention of one of the museum attendants.

"Quite authentic, isn't it?" asked the attendant.

"I'm counting on it," murmured Turner.

"Pardon me, Sir?"

"I'm sorry. Were you speaking with me?" Turner tried to cover up for the comment he had made under his breath.

The attendant continued, "Yes, I said it's quite authentic."

"So I've heard. Are onlookers allowed to view the inside of the craft?" Turner questioned.

"Yes, as long as an attendant accompanies you. If you'd like to see the inside, I can show you now."

Turner answered, "Yes, please."

The two of them walked to the far side of the shuttle where the side entry door was located. The attendant took out his key and opened the door.

"As you can see, the thickness of the doors and side panels were proven quite effective. If NASA had only been able to develop a better power supply, this shuttle vehicle could have traveled indefinitely."

They both entered the control area of the shuttle from the cargo area where they had boarded. Turner's eyes were like a camera as they focused on the control panels surrounding the two high backed seats in a semicircular fashion. The attendant was explaining a few of the controls and gauges, but Turner's mind was all but ignoring him. Instead, he was mentally modifying the controls to adapt to equipment they had decided would be needed for their trek.

The attendant continued, "Yes, a fine space craft; one of three and the only one we have on display here."

Turner was brought out of his silent planning. "Pardon me, you said one of three? I was told this was the only shuttle rebuilt?"

"It was at first; but, the NASA Museum Foundation ran into some financial problems and when they were told of a small number of antique collectors who were interested in placing a shuttle into their own displays, it was an answer to their financial straits."

"Are these other shuttles intact - complete?"

"Yes Sir. They are identical to this one."

"I suppose the other two shuttles have already been purchased?"

"One has indeed been sold, but the other shuttle has just been completed and made available for sale."

"This is incredible! I, too, have sought for just such a display for my collection. I must speak immediately with whomever is responsible for selling the other shuttle."

The attendant looked as if he were celebrating Christmas. "My supervisor is here now and will be able to contact the Foundation today, if you like? Of course, Sir, I've taken for granted you can afford the one billion dollar price tag for the shuttle?"

"In fact, my friend, if your supervisor can arrange to have the shuttle delivered to my designated location within the week, I'll make sure he receives an additional million dollars for the purchase."

"Yes Sir! I'll inform him immediately!"

The surprised attendant hurriedly walked out of the shuttle and over to the museum offices. Turner sat down in one of the pilot's seats and leaned back laughing under his breath while slowly moving his hands across the control panels.

With all of the excitement welled up inside of Turner, it seemed to take a very short time for him to return home. When he arrived, Sara was not in her apartment; so. Turner began studying the schematics and blueprints of the shuttle given to him by the overjoyed museum supervisor.

It had been two months since the shuttle replica had been delivered to the large country barn that had once served one of the farming conglomerates. The barn had been used to store the equipment needed to farm the conglomerate's 2000 acres, which provided ample space to house and prepare the shuttle. During the past two months, the work on the shuttle had turned into an endless maze of new discoveries and needed modifications.

It was early in the morning when Turner heard a knock at the barn's front door. He cautiously went to discover Professor Solmon waiting to enter. Turner quickly stepped out to greet the Professor, making sure he could not see inside the storage barn.

"Professor! What a surprise!"

"Turner, I'm not one to waste words. I knew when you and Sara first visited me with your questions concerning the old NASA project what your intentions were. I've come to help."

"Help? I'm not sure I understand Professor."

"You must streamline your time, Turner. For instance, if you would let me in to see your proposed escape ship, I could begin assisting the two of you in the necessary modifications and additions needed to make the antiquated craft escape worthy."

Turner was silent as the professor pushed him aside and stepped into the shuttle's storage barn. "Ah, it is magnificent. What have you done so far? Better yet, let me look."

For days, both Turner and Sara worked more silently than before because of the surprise addition to their team. They were very happy with his assistance since the vastness of his expertise had proven invaluable within the first few days. The time went more smoothly when they became comfortable with his presence. The two of them had worked alone for so long, they had almost excluded the rest of humanity.

The most valuable of the initial additions initiated by the professor was a perpetual emissions element he created as a proposed power supply for space travel before all programs were ceased in lieu of other Council directives. This power supply could provide the shuttle's existing engines with enough energy to propel them at 90% the speed of light for a nearly indefinite period of time. Until this addition made by the professor, an alternate source of power had not been available.

Each day, the professor had a different computer component delivered to their barn for the three of them to install into the shuttle. After installing the individual units, the professor programmed them through the use of a micro-sonic input unit, of his own design, to aid in the efficient networking of the individual components.

During their three months of working together, the three of them had become very close. An attitude of family togetherness had been created through their team effort towards survival. As they grew together, they began sharing often through their work efforts. As their relationship matured and their conversations becoming more open, they began discussing what to name their ship. It was an easy decision, capped off with a rowdy "here-here" by the professor as they christened their shuttle the *Exodus* – a label they cherished and prayed for as a successful name for what they were planning on as their refuge from definite doom.

Each day, the Sun appeared brighter with a steadily growing glow of eerie white. The wind had increased over the day before, but it was much appreciated since the temperature was unusually hot.

Turner and Sara were working early today on some of the numerous final adjustments to the shuttle's inner structure. On this day especially, they felt confident about their plan of escape. The professor had not yet arrived this morning. He was usually an earlier riser than his two younger comrades. Turner and Sara agreed they would not trouble him with a wake-up call and just let him rest as long as he wanted this morning. The work was going well and they had calculated there was still six to eight weeks before their leaving would be necessary.

All of the technical propulsion and guidance systems were installed and tested; all of the computers and sensors had been programmed by the professor as a storehouse of the majority of Earth's accumulated knowledge. The professor had even installed a protective compartment to store several classic books from his personal library, including his prized possession, a practically new Bible sealed in an air-tight acrylic package two hundred years before the professor lucked upon it.

The only remaining tasks to complete were those designed by the three of them for comfort. But, even with the vast size of the shuttle's now restructured cargo compartment, the amount of space remaining for these comfort modifications was minimal. This was mainly due to the scores of additional computers and the hug food supply stored in the cargo hold.

"Turner, we still haven't decided where we're going to relocate. With our power supply, we can travel indefinitely, but we won't be traveling more than 85 to 90% the speed of light. At that speed we're about four years from the nearest star system."

"I know Sara. Time will be against us while we're in space; but Sara, that's still more years we'll have – even if we're living on the shuttle, it's still living."

This had been Turner's train of thought all along. He knew space travel was still out of reach for star travel. He also knew there was no real choice. On Earth there was no chance. While in space, there was at least a thread of a chance to continue their lives.

The wind was much stronger now. The old barn that surrounded the shuttle's launching berth creaked as the warm winds screamed past the weakening walls. An occasional look of wonder mixed with apprehension poured over both of the faces while they continued to work.

The barn, once full of crates and boxes of material and equipment for the shuttle, now housed only the craft itself. The engine housing firmly rested against the protruding platform of the slanted, below ground ramp. The cockpit nose of the Exodus pointed defiantly upward at a step 45 degree angle towards the sky it already seem to be reaching for. The elevation ramp the shuttle rested on was designed to increase their angle to a full 90 degrees when their departure date arrived. The elevation of the ramp, they felt, was a crucial part of their lift off.

"Turner, I think I hear the professor ringing the entry sound. I'll go to let him in the barn."

Sara left the Exodus to meet the professor only to see him in a most excited, frantic, and frightened condition.

"Sara, where is Turner? We have no time left! We must leave now! Get into the craft."

"Professor, what are you saying? What happened?"

"I'll explain inside! We must board Exodus and prepare for lift-off."

The professor ran to the boarding ramp followed closely by Sara who was dumbfounded by his remarks. As she entered, the professor stopped and secured the shuttle's air locked entry door.

"Turner! Come to the control room now!"

"Professor. Are you alright?" Turner asked as he arrived to the cockpit control area only to find the professor already activating the propulsion and operations computer switches as he spoke.

"Turner, Sara, we were wrong. Our calculations on the timing of the atmospheric burn-through were incorrect by nearly two months. The atmosphere, it's collapsing, even as we're standing here. Haven't you noticed the increase in the winds? The earth is beginning to break apart."

"Oh my God, Professor, can we still make it?" questioned Turner, as he began to hurriedly help activate their shuttle controls. The once calm confidence now changed to desperation. Then turner almost yelled, "I'll go to the back and secure the airtight hatches."

"Hurry, Turner! We must try to leave in sixty minutes, no more!" commanded the professor.

Working as quickly as he could, Turner had secured the cargo hold's hatches and returned to the pilot's chair with no wasted steps.

No one talked as they worked in their respective areas hoping for success in their now doubtful escape. Turner sat on the edge of the pilot's chair checking and adjusting switches and controls while waiting for the engines to warm sufficiently for firing. Sara sat on his right in the copilot's chair monitoring and adjusting the overhead controls to assure the proper angle for their lift-off from the elevation platform.

"I'm firing the engines, Sara, increase our angle to the full 90 degree stance. Professor, belt in. In three minutes it's full power!"

No sooner had Turner finished when the bam exploded away from the slowly elevating shuttle. The winds increased so devastatingly the three could see entire houses flying above them.

The elevation unit moved very slowly under the great weight of the gleaming ship. Sara was carefully monitoring the angle indicator when a house that sat nearly one hundred yards from the bam site was lifted by the winds, foundation and all, and hurled against the elevation generator, forcing it to tear away from the elevation platform and causing the platform to crash against the ground with the shuttle still attached.

"Are you two okay?" shouted Turner but not waiting for a reply. "Sara, release the shuttle's holding bolts from the platform; we'll have to try it from ground level. I'm switching the engines to full power!"

The shuttle slowly crept off the platform and began moving down the small country road which was already scarred by hundreds of small cracks in the Earth's crust as the enveloping force of the protective atmosphere was giving way to the vacuum nature of the once separated darkness of space. The control stick quivered fiercely in Turner's right hand as his left hand slowly increased the throttle.

The shuttle had become slightly airborne. The professor stared with awe at the ominous view forming hastily ahead of the craft. Sara was leaning fully back in her chair with her eyes stretched open to their limit and clutching both arm rests with a grip of impending doom.

"Full ascension now, Turner! We must ascend now," pleaded the professor.

"The shuttle can't take it; our speed isn't great enough; she'll stall!"

"If you don't ascend now. Turner, we'll become part of this explosion. It's our only chance. Ascend now!"

No reply from Turner except for pulling back his hand control followed by the lowering of the horizon as the shuttle's nose rose to an upright direction. The craft jerked roughly as the strain on the engines was added to by the pressure of the ascent.

Then, all at once, a deafening sound consisting of one single, awful tone pressed against their eardrums until they could feel the blood from their ears slowly rolling down their faces to their necks. They felt the shuttle shake and shake until they each leaned back onto their chairs and closed their eyes. They knew death had caught them as well as their planet. Turner felt they had all been pointlessly fooling themselves about the now failed escape. Turner reached out his right hand, taking it off the control stick, towards Sara, whose left hand was outstretched towards him.

The two hands clasped as they blacked out under the incredible G force increasing rapidly from the Earth's exploding force.

The professor was more frightened than he had ever been before; but, a feeling of contentment slowly enveloped his mind, because of the attempt he had been a part of, to at least try to continue life in the face of now guaranteed death. He too then, with his contentment, blacked out.

The darkness of space, peppered with fragments of what had been the Earth, now received the explosion scared Exodus which miraculously survived the ordeal. Its passengers had also survived but were yet unconscious. Faint beats were methodically resounding from the computers and guidance systems fully activated prior to the explosion.

Turner began to awaken and said, "My head. Oh, the ship! We're still in the ship!" He turned to Sara who was still unconscious and felt the pulsing flow from within her left wrist. The pulse beat was strong as was the professor's. Turner began studying the system control panels to discover what damage may have been caused by the explosion.

"It's amazing! Everything is still in good working condition. I'll check the other computers."

Even though back-up computers were brought along as replacements the knowledge stored within them was now irreplaceable. Turner moved to the rear of the control area, sat in the operator's chair, and activated several of the recall switches.

"Good. The system appears intact. I wonder...?"

He noticed one of the circuits set in the record mode.

"Do you suppose the professor..." he continued to question himself.

Reaching for the switch, Turner activated it and saw the professor's face filling on the screen. He sat back in surprise to view the unexpected development.

"My name is Solomon, Professor Solomon. My friends and I have embarked on a project to escape the inevitable destruction of our home, the planet Earth, the third planet from the Sun in our solar system."

"This record is being compiled automatically by these computers previously connected to the largest local broadcasting station on our side of the planet. These computers will record the actual reactions and activities surrounding the destruction of Earth by the contaminated solar winds from our Sun. I'm not sure any of us will survive; but, this record should serve to enable science, whatever science may exist in other parts of the galaxy, to study and be made aware of this part of history."

The professor's image left the screen and after only a couple of seconds, a chain of news broadcasts began appearing starting only five days before their leaving Earth.

"It's been over a month since the report came from every country around the world that the temperatures had risen to record marks above 110 degrees. This included a report from the northern arctic area. An official spokesman of the Council has denied any possibility of danger as a result of some unpublished nuclear testing or anything for that matter; but, as far as this reporter's opinion, something is deadly wrong!"

"There's so much happening that is going unexplained. There are heat-related deaths by the thousands as well as unexpected and devastating earthquakes, tidal waves, hurricanes and many other so called act-of-God occurrences combined to cause over four million deaths over the last six months."

"This reporter is extremely frightened!"

Turner was captivated and surprised. He and his fellow escapees had taken no time to follow the events around the world since they were so busy readying the Exodus for its journey. They had no idea the deaths and catastrophes were so great in number.

As he sat for hours in front of the viewing screen, his feelings became mixed. On one hand he felt fortunate to have escaped the holocaust when so many perished; but, on the other hand, he became scared-scared they had not really survived but had only delayed the inevitable.

When the last of the recorded broadcasts ended abruptly, Turner lowered his head to his hands and cried. The sadness in his heart was nearly unbearable.

Meanwhile, the professor had also regained consciousness and for the past several minutes had been watching the computer's view screen over Turner's shoulder.

He spoke softly, "Turner, I'm happy that you're alive."

"Professor, did you see?"

"Yes, I decided it would be science-worthy even though I was sure it would be tragically sad. We must awaken Sara. If you'll do that Turner, there's something I want to show you both."

Turner did return to the front of the control area where Sara lay sleeping. She was easily awakened by Turner followed by an emotional embrace of joy in finding her love was still alive. They sat and glared out the front viewing window at the bright stars resting so very far away from them, separated by the pure darkness of space.

It was a beautiful sight. Hand in hand, conversation about its beauty felt soothing to Turner as the professor returned from retrieving a book from the cargo area.

"Turner, Sara, I've re-read a few passages of this Bible and I..."

"Bible," questioned Sara. "Why? What's going on?"

"Sara," Turner explained, "the professor and I know now of the tragic devastation that occurred prior to our leaving Earth."

"That's right, Sara," continued the professor. "There are passages in this book that were called prophecy, or the telling of things to come. I believe what happened to the Earth was prophesied over two thousand years before it happened and we were caught up in what the theologians had labeled the rapture."

"The rapture? But..."

"Let me continue," requested the professor. "We left a planet being destroyed by fire, and by unsurpassed natural disasters. Plus, there were millions who did not die with the planet, but were killed, or taken, as it were, before the actual destruction. We are examples of that, except us, unlike others of our planet, escaped with our lives. It must be for a reason; one we'll probably never know."

"You really see this as a possibility Professor?" questioned Turner.

"Not only a possibility, but the most believable probability. Nevertheless, we're here and alive; we must continue on as planned. We must remain with the living since for some reason our lives have been saved."

And so it was for the three of them. They began life of study and growing together while being carried by their craft towards the closest star to the Sun, Proxima Centuri. Proxima was the third star in the Alpha Centuri system.

The Centuri system was by far the closest star system in the Local group of the Milky Way galaxy. Its distance was only 4.3 light years and Proxima, due to its orbital motion around the first and second stars of the system, was in fact nearly a light year closer to the Earth at one point in its orbit. The professor's calculations had shown their journey would take nearly four years since their speed was continuously very near the speed of light. This was why astronomers of the old Earth had named the star Proxima.

The professor spent nearly all of the first six months setting up a portion of the cargo area for his telescope assembly. With this, he hoped to study and photograph the stars as they had never been photographed before. His discoveries were as gifts from God due to their magnitude and their previously unknown existence. He had never been as happy as he found himself becoming; floating in his observatory next to the stars.

The area the professor created in the cargo hold was in the most forward point near the control area. He and Turner reasoned this placement would be wise because this location would enable the professor to monitor the control area while carrying on his stellar explorations.

A thirty-inch telescope was mounted in the center of the area with an incredibly clear skylight covering the entire area used by the professor. This skylight was as all of the skylights attached to the Exodus, equipped with retractable metal shields that were closed when a skylight was not in use. Surrounding the telescope were computers and spectrographic analyzers of various shapes and functions.

To have all of this equipment for study along with being so much closer to those stars being studied without any atmospheric disturbances blocking or distorting the lighted images was truly a utopia for any serious astronomer.

Sara had also been working on an area of her own. She'd built a separation wall to close off the farthest back portion of the cargo area and decorated it as a private living quarters for her and Turner. Soft carpeting, an artificial fireplace along one of the walls and with two large skylights: one overhead and the second on the wall opposite the fireplace.

The centerpiece of the living area was a large ten-foot by fifteen foot floor-level bed covered with several plush cushions. This room was calming to both Turner and Sara. It afforded them the privacy and the most romantic view ever seen from any bedroom in the universe.

Turner had also been busy in the cargo area. He had constructed an enclosed hothouse styled garden of various vegetables started from the seeds he had brought with him from Earth. He began seeing a tremendous growth pattern from all of the vegetables planted and had discovered the lack of resistance from gravity allowed each plant more upward growth and ease in fully developing under the lamps of simulated light.

When the garden reached maturity, Turner began to prepare special vegetable dishes for each of their meals. A treat for people floating in space somewhere between the Sun and Proxima.

Proxima was clearly in view now though reaching it was still another light year in the future. The Exodus had functioned flawlessly for its now three-year journey.

Turner and Sara had been quite happy for the first three and a half years of their married lives. They spent most of their evenings in their private quarters learning more about each other and becoming stronger in their love.

"Sara, come over here for a while," Turner motioned for Sara to join him on the floor-level bed. She walked to the bed's edge and crawled over to Turner's side.

"You're more beautiful today than when we first met. How long has it been? Even with all this we've been through it seems like such a short time."

"Turner, I've never really asked this; but, when you requested our marriage from the Council that day, did you love me then or has it been since then?"

"You're trying to get me into trouble, aren't you? Well, I can remember vividly that it was two years before when I realized I was in love with you. You remember when we had that picnic at the conservation park and the whole group played that game that Frederick bad read about in the history of sports and athletics he found at the archives called Football?"

"Sure, you were really quite good at that. I remember you tackled more people than anyone else."

"Sara, do you remember who it was I tackled the most? It was you. I knew the rules were broken when I tackled you since you never carried the ball. That was also the reason I never let you up immediately; it was my chance to be next to you."

"And all along, Turner, I thought I was the lucky one since you came near me so often. I was more excited about you that day than I had been about any man in my entire life! But Turner, on a few of those plays, did you have to hit me so hard?"

"Well Sara that was the point of the game. As I remember, you hit awfully hard yourself."

"You mean like this..." Sara then took one of the cushions in her hands and began to beat Turner on his head and shoulders laughing and repeating, "Like this and like this!"

Both she and Turner engaged in the cushion battle with laughter and comical slurs until Turner took Sara by the shoulders, pressed her down to the bed and stopped fighting while on his hands and knees looking down at her until her eyes caught his.

"I love you, Sara," whispered Turner with cherished sincerity as he lowered his lips towards hers.

Just before he kissed her, Sara replied, "I love you, my darling Turner."

Their hands caressed and lips kissed one another; the passion was real and very loving. They hardly moved from that position as they continued their exchange of soft touching, yearning whimpers, and tender contact between their lips.

"Turner, Sara," spoke the professor's voice over the intercom, "I think you'd both better come to the control area." Professor Solomon tried hard to make his request without emotion. While his two friends were in their private quarters, professor detected something on the sensor panels. He didn't want to disturb them until he was sure. As the object came into view, the professor said, "It's nearly impossible."

When the two joined the professor, they were stunned at the sight now clearly visible.

"Is it possible?" questioned Turner.

"It's possible, Turner," replied the professor; "but I think it very unlikely there's anyone alive."

Floating just ahead of their replica of the twentieth century shuttle craft was what appeared to be one of the originals. It was identical to the Exodus in appearance, but was twice as large since the Exodus was a scaled-down replica. Badly scarred and showing no signs of movement other than a slight gravitational motion towards Proxima of no more than a few thousand miles an hour, the newly discovered shuttle appeared to be dead.

The professor had slowed the Exodus down from the moment he had detected the object on the sensors. The Exodus now hovered just above its predecessor matching its crawling pace.

"Any radio signals coming from the craft, Sara?"

"No, Turner. There are some noises coming from the inside though. They're garbled and I can't tell if they're equipment or people. I'm going to transmit a message to them and see if they're receiving, or for that matter alive."

Sara began transmitting a voice signal saying, "NASA shuttle, please identify yourselves; NASA shuttle, please identify yourselves."

She attempted this message for five minutes adjusting the signal modulation each time to insure each possible frequency would be attempted.

"Turner," began Sara, "I'm getting no reply on any frequency. I would guess they've been dead for some time now.

"I'm not sure we have a choice at this point," spoke the professor in a low, solemn tone. "We must board her to find out for sure whether or not there is anyone left alive. I for one could not sleep at night thinking there could be even one person left alive on that dead ship whose only chance to continue living flew off without searching."

"You're right Professor," agreed Turner. Sara and I will board the shuttle while you monitor the controls so our ship doesn't float away from us."

The professor set and locked the Exodus into a simulated gravitational connection with the second shuttle as Turner and Sara suited up for their short but still dangerous spacewalk.

Turner and Sara entered the Exodus' decompression room that led to the exit hatch. Once the room had been vacuumed, to match the void of space resting just the other side of the doorway, Turner activated the door and it opened. When it finally opened, Sara held what looked like a large flare gun and fired it at the antique shuttle. The gun fired a safety line from the Exodus to the second shuttle that would adhere itself to the outer wall of the vessel thus allowing the two of them a means to navigate their space walk with the utmost precaution.

The trek across was easy and it brought them directly to the entry hatch where they would gain access to the ship. It was quite a stroke of luck this craft was of identical design to their own. This advantage gave them a confident knowledge they would not encounter any unexpected structural problems with their entry.

As they reached the outer wall of the vessel, Sara pulled a small device from her space suit pocket and attached it to the outer portion of the opening mechanism, thus giving them a key to the door. While she was doing this, Turner was prying the cover panel off of the electronic hatch opening mechanism to allow Sara to complete her task.

"Turner," spoke Sara, "this switch will automatically open and shut this hatch each five minutes. This means going in and coming out we'll have to wait that period of time inside the decompression chamber. That should be just enough time for the room to change its pressure both entering and leaving."

The door opened. Slowly the two entered the small compression chamber. Everything appeared as they expected as the two peered through the small doorway window into the cargo area while waiting for the room's pressure to change and allow them entry.

After the two had embarked on their search aboard the second shuttle, the professor was contemplating how it would have been to have traveled on the now ancient relic. He was trying to imagine how long the ship had been in space and why? A journey of this kind, that is to say one of such a long distance, was thought to be impossible during the years of the original shuttle program. It was not only the slow speeds of travel, possible twenty-five to thirty thousand miles an hour, but most importantly the impossibility of being able to carry enough fuel for such a venture.

The professor's eternal emissions fuel not only lasted virtually forever and only required a small area for its storage in the engine room, but it also enabled the newly designed craft to travel as near the speed of light as the historic theory of relativity would allow-some six million miles an hour at top speed.

The professor now brought his mind back to concentrating on the journey of his two comrades as he saw the bright spotlights from the Exodus being reflected from the flight scarred shuttle Turner and Sara had just entered.

As soon as the outer hatch closed, Turner began to bring the pressure of the tiny passageway up to the level of the pressure inside of the ship.

"This is a good sign Sara. If there was no oxygen inside the ship it would be impossible to pressurize this chamber."

"I suppose the slowness of the entering pressure is due to the weakness of the inside pressure. That's understandable, but you must hurry Turner; we only have one minute before the outer hatch will open again."

The inner hatch opened, the two quickly stepped inside, and hurriedly closed the inner hatch between them. None too soon either, since the moment it sealed, the outer hatch re-opened and the compartment pressure release caused a small swooshing sound as it escaped into the vacuum of space.

"Are you two alright?" signaled the professor. "I heard the pressure release."

"We're fine, Professor. Keep the circuit open; we're heading for the front control area."

The cargo area was huge - it looked like a warehouse, especially with all the crates scattered throughout the area. As they moved slowly through the cargo hold, both Sara and Turner studied the labeling and the dates on each crate. Names like "DuPont", McDonald-Douglas and "NASA" were stamped on the fronts of the crates along with one of two dates, 2040 and 2041.

Some of the crates had been opened properly, most looked smashed open. Turner was guessing the original shuttle they were in had been through some tremendously turbulent activity causing not only the bum scars on the outer hull but also the cargo being found in shambles. Both Sara and Turner walked slowly, being cautious not to disturb any of the cargo and cause further disarray.

"The living quarters are just beyond that door Sara. Let's get this over with," spoke Turner with great apprehension.

Turner activated the door release and they entered the corridor to find the bodies of four crew members. Each one had a knife stuck directly through their heart.

"Turner! What could have happened?"

Then Turner heard a noise from the control area.

"Did you hear that Sara? Let's move on, but stay cautious."

They moved to the access door to the control room, opened it hurriedly to find a seemingly half-dead man sitting in the pilot's chair talking quietly to himself. Turner called out to the man, "Are you alright?"

The man turned and spoke. "We all should have died with the Earth. It was meant to be and we tampered with Providence."

"Sara," whispered Turner, "the man has obviously gone insane; be careful."

The man continued as if he hardly noticed Turner and Sara were strangers to him. "I was sure we would have died long ago, but I kept quiet. I couldn't stay quiet any longer though when the fifth one died of natural causes at fifty years of age - she was only fifty!"

Turner spoke, "How many were originally on ship?"

"On ship," the man repeated, "on ship, we started with ten healthy twenty year olds and five died of heart attacks at only fifty."

"You said five," questioned Turner, "what about the other four and yourself?"

"I couldn't take it any longer!" cried the man. "I knew we should have died with the Earth; so, so I killed them. They're happier now. They're where they should be rather than floating out here between heaven and hell."

The man's voice was almost childlike as he explained his deeds as a child would to parent when caught doing something wrong.

"Soon I'll die," continued the man. "The cuts on my wrist will see to that. Then there's this flying death trap. Soon it will die too."

"What!" exclaimed Turner to the man. "What do you mean soon it will die too?"

"The bomb," continued the man, "Oh, I didn't tell you about the bomb?"

The man's speech was becoming very slow and slurred as death continued its near victory. "There's a rather effective bomb set to kill this beast in less than five minutes when I, when I...OH GOD!!"

"Turner, he's dead. Let's get out of here!"

"You first and run Sara, run!"

The two ran back through the living quarters and down the corridor to the cargo hold. As they ran through the cargo area Turner was yelling instructions to Sara.

"Sara, I'll activate the compression hatch and you go through first, get outside the ship and tell the professor to make the Exodus ready for a full speed."

When they reached the hatch, the outer door had just closed. This enabled Sara to enter the decompression chamber immediately as Turner closed the inner hatch and made the room a virtual vacuum so Sara could escape to the outside of the ship. The room was readied just in time for the automatic switch to open the outer hatch for Sara's escape. When she completely cleared the doorway, Turner saw the outer door had closed.

Turner, after readjusting the decompression gauge to ready the room for his own escape, opened the inner door and entered the chamber himself. He realized he had put his own life in jeopardy to save Sara's by allowing her to go out first; but it was not possible to decompress the escape chamber from inside the room itself. Those controls only had the capability to recompress the atmosphere in order to enter the ship. He also realized standing inside the chamber it would still be another four minutes before the automatic switch would reopen the outer hatch.

"Sara," yelled Turner over his own communicator as she was now half-way between the two shuttles on her way to the Exodus, "It's going to take too long for me to get out of here. You and the professor must get the Exodus cleared from the explosion or we'll all die!"

Sara had made it back to the Exodus and was already inside the decompression chamber.

"We can't leave you Turner!" yelled Sara, "we'll wait!"

"No!" demanded Turner. "You must be saved Sara! You must leave now! You heard me too, Professor, leave now!"

The engines started to slowly move the ship. Sara was crying and gazing out of the hatch for only a moment as she waved her last goodbye to Turner.

At that moment, after Sara had sat down inside the compartment, the outer hatch of the death-destined shuttle opened allowing Turner to escape and barely grasp onto one of the crossing cables that had severed itself from the old shuttle. Turner secured the cable around his waist as the Exodus started its own escape.

The old shuttle was almost enveloped into the darkness of space when Turner, who was firmly attached to the Exodus by the safety cable, had to cover his eyes to shield them from the explosion's fiery brilliance.

Turner was slowly making his way forward on the topside of the Exodus towards the entry hatch of the compression chamber. When he reached it, he could see Sara through the window sitting on a stool with her head in her hands feverishly crying over losing Turner.

Turner knocked hard against the door, which to Sara sounded like a very light tap. When she lifted her head and saw his face through the hatch window, she exclaimed, "Turner, you're alive!"

Then Turner said, "Open the door, Sara, I promise to be good!"

Turner was trying hard to joke and cover his fear. He had been faced with almost certain death and again, somehow, was saved. Puzzled, but relieved, Turner slept well that evening.

It had been nearly three months since the encounter with the second mysterious shuttle. At first, the three talked a lot about the surprising discovery; but, as time went on, a solemn silence about the matter took over and no one talked of it or even referenced it in the slightest. There seemed to be thoughts generated by the occurrence no one would vocalize, but it seemed likely all three dwelt heavily on these thoughts.

The three months had been a dangerously busy span of time. Twice they had to shut down the Exodus' power plant to repair the engines. On one of the two occasions, it took all three of them two days of work outside the craft to repair the angle of one of the jet cones that had been damaged by some sort of storm consisting of rocks and stones of all shapes and sizes. Most were too small to do any damage, but one struck the cone broadside and virtually closed it shut, causing a potential feedback of the power plant emitter.

Other repairs were necessary during the three-month period. Two of the guidance computers became irreparable and in need of replacement. They all felt grateful the professor had enough foresight to bring extra computers for this very possibility.

The occurrences were taxing mentally and physically on all three. The professor took it the best, though, possibly due to years of combined successes and failures while on Earth.

Turner remained quiet about the whole situation successfully holding the tension inside. Sara was quite another story. She went through periods of forgetfulness and slight memory loss. Turner and the professor discussed her several times while she was sleeping. The professor had studied Psychology as a second undergraduate degree, as was required by the Council, and felt she was going to have to completely address the intensely pent-up feelings or she would soon succumb so completely to the stress that Turner nor the professor would be able to help her. They decided to induce just such a reaction.

Turner sat next to Sara on the relaxing lounge at the rear of the control area and started the piercing conversation.

"Sara, have you ever thought of how you'll die?" These words seemed to be the hardest words Turner had ever spoken. He knew the reaction was to be painful to Sara but necessary.

"Die," she replied in a surprised tone. "That's all I've been thinking about. That seems to be all we have left."

"Sara, surely you don't believe that," interjected the professor, softly stepping quietly into the control area from the cargo room.

"You too, huh," spoke Sara. "Well, you both may be able to cope with this lingering death; but I can't! At first I was appalled by the crewmember of that shuttle killing the others, but now I see it as an act of love for them. Don't you see? We're all as good as dead. I've nearly lost you Turner too many times to this God-forsaken darkness."

Sara was now staring at the ceiling, becoming very agitated and with her clenched fists slowly began pounding the seat she was sitting on and continued to talk.

"We don't belong out here! We should have died on Earth! Turner, I'm scared! Help me! I'm dying!"

Sara jumped to her feet and began running through the ship towards the engine room.

When Turner caught Sara, she was beginning to activate the escape hatch screaming, "I can't breathe! I can't breathe!"

Meanwhile the professor had readied a tranquilizing injection for their troubled friend. Turner was holding her as she cried, "I don't know what's happening to me Turner. I'm the only one of us this emptiness is bothering. Turner, am I completely mad?"

"No Sara, my love," compassionately replied Turner, "you're not mad. You're just in pain as both the professor and I are. Sara, you've been unable to release the pain and it's been eating at you like a cancer."

She had Turner in a desperate clinch she would not release. Turner continued to console her as they walked towards their private room. Like a baby, Sara continued to mumble, "I'm sorry I acted up. I'll feel better tomorrow."

"Sara," spoke the professor, "this injection is only a mild sedative. It'll help you sleep tonight and I'm sure you will feel better tomorrow."

After the injection, Sara appeared relaxed, separated from the few frightening moments just before. She rested well that evening. This also appeared to be the beginning of the release she had so seriously needed.

"Turner," spoke the professor, "don't feel badly about causing these emotions of Sara's to emerge. She reacted exactly as I had hoped she would. She blew off the steam both of us have felt ourselves."

"You're right Professor. There have been moments when I found myself agreeing with the execution method used on the other shuttle."

Months went by and strength again was seen in Sara's character. But still, as with all three, the control of the subconscious pain and unspoken agony only seemingly postponed any further outburst that could lead to losing control totally.

"Turner, Sara, I've finished the calculations we've been hoping for."

"Well, Professor, what's the answer?" begged Turner. "Is there a planet orbiting Proxima that might be inhabitable?"

"Yes Turner," replied the professor, "there are two planets in fact, that orbit Proxima at a safe enough distance that a temperature acceptable to us to exist of about 75 degrees year round. We couldn't hope for better."

They were only days away from the calculated orbital entry point around the first of the two planets and ten hours in front of Proxima itself. Each of the three were sitting in front of monitoring panels, checking and rechecking the constant flow of new data being fed into the computers by meters and radio telescopes about the star Proxima as they grew close and made ready to pass by it.

The information they felt was most important was the temperatures emitted from the star. The higher the suspected temperature, the greater the course adjustment needed to insure a safe distance for the Exodus as it passed by the long sought after light in the sky.

The second part of this was the professor had reasoned the closer to the star they would be able to travel as they passed, the fewer course adjustments and corrections to arrive at Proxima's first planet.

"Professor," spoke Sara, "the light meters are reading direct temperatures from Proxima now. You can switch to C-3 on your control board to view it on your screen."

"Yes," replied the professor, "the temperatures at the most crucial point is very low. We can adjust our course to travel even closer to Proxima than our present course has us heading. With this adjustment, we'll be crossing the path of Proxima at a 40 degree angle and be heading directly for its first planet."

"A 40 degree angle, Professor," questioned Turner, "that will bring us very close to the Star's corona."

"There's no problem with that Turner," replied the professor. "The temperature at that point will only cause acceptable levels of heat to be created on the outer hull of the Exodus."

"Professor," spoke Sara, "the gravitational sensing panels are showing an unusual pattern of magnetic disturbances just ahead, in fact, at the very point we'll begin passing Proxima."

"Recheck the readings Sara," ordered Turner as he sat in the pilot's chair and monitored the guidance panels.

He also noticed variances on the guidance sensors as they neared their pass-by maneuver with Proxima.

"Turner," began Sara, "these readings are accurate. The disturbance is there."

"You've got to be more specific, Sara!" demanded Turner. "What are the disturbances and where do they emanate?"

"I can define them as spiraling magnetic waves, Turner; and their not only spiraling, but they are also rotating around Proxima itself."

"How wide is the pattern?" questioned Turner. "Can we go around them?"

"No, it's too late, Turner. We're about to enter them in less than sixty seconds."

"Alright, in our seats, now! We'll have to fly through this one. Prepare for the worst..." were the last words spoken by any of the three prior to their entry into this strange gravitationally magnetic field.

As the Exodus entered the field it began to tremble. The ship's speed was steady, just below light speed as it entered the field, but after only five minutes inside the field it was registering five times that and rapidly increasing.

The ship now was orbiting around Proxima nearly ten times the speed of light. The three were motionless in their seats as they saw a frightening display of flashing lights and fire through the forward window. Turner had been studying the navigational meters since the entry into the field and the subsequent high-speed orbital trap that had caught the Exodus. He had seen that they had traveled on a counter clock-wise direction nearly thirty times around Proxima; and also that the Exodus was being pulled further and further into the flaming chromosphere of the now deadly star.

He reasoned they only had one chance to save themselves from the clutches of the star's grip. That was to attempt a full ninety-degree turn of the Exodus and thus, hopefully, free them from their orbital doom. He also reasoned it could tear the Exodus in half; but, they had no more time. The force had now caused thirty-two orbits at speeds above 10 times that of light.

With no warning, Turner threw the directional guidance into the manual control mode, grasped the stick firmly with both hands and pulled sharply to the right.

The ship now shook with earthquake-like tremors. The deadly picture from the forward window began changing somewhat and with such a pattern Turner realized he had thrown them into a high-speed spin. The spinning ship nevertheless was becoming free of the falling motion but the speed was increasing.

The picture now was completely different as the Exodus was freed completely from Proxima's grip, but was still spinning clockwise with tremendously high revolutions and flying through space so much faster than the ten times the speed of light it had been flying at during its orbital battle with Proxima that the velocity measuring circuits shorted and sparked like miniature lightning bolts bouncing across the panels. Other circuits could not stand the strain, as was evidenced by their exploding and shorting out all over the control area. Turner had long stopped monitoring the meters and concentrated his full strength in trying to pull the now seemingly locked far right position of the guidance stick towards the left and thus hopefully end the spinning motion of the Exodus' whirling through space.

It had been over an hour since the Exodus freed itself from Proxima. To Turner it had seemed like millions of years of pulling hard left on the stick with no success; now though, he felt a hint of give from the impregnable locked position of the stick. He kept pulling.

Sara had said nothing and had sat motionless through the entire ordeal; only moaning and crying from fright. The professor had tucked his head away from view onto his chest. Turner later discovered the professor had suffered severe pain from a fatal heart attack when the Exodus had begun orbiting Proxima at its great speeds. Due to Turner's preoccupation with the control stick and Sara's total withdrawal from reality and eventually passing out the professor's death had gone unnoticed.

Turner felt more flexibility in the control stick and he noticed the swirling revolutions were coming to a halt. Slowly the craft came back into Turner's control, with a straight heading towards what appeared to be Earth!

"It can't be! There's no possible...!"

Turner now noticed the land configurations below as Earth. Not only that, but the Exodus was very near the outermost part of the Earth's atmosphere. Turner pulled on the stick to steer away from the planet he had seen completely destroyed but as he did, the entire guidance control panel shorted and threw sparks and flame all across the front of the control area.

The Exodus began to re-enter the Earth's atmosphere. The flames on the outer hull of the nearly destroyed craft caused the inner walls of the ship to become extremely hot and give off a slight cloud of smoke. Turner saw the Exodus was gliding through a sky of royal blue only slightly contrasted from the glistening ocean below.

Moments later, Turner realized the Exodus was nearly ready to fall into the ocean only seconds before had appeared so peaceful. He held tightly to the arms of his chair as the shell of a ship they had named Exodus crashed into the Atlantic.

I remember that day vividly now. I pulled Sara out of the sinking shuttle as I said farewell to the professor. Still unconscious, Sara was otherwise physically unharmed. She had, though, completely lost her memory; and, based on all that happened I thought it best to leave her ignorant of the past.

When I reached shore and sought help, I was informed of the date from a man who lived along the beach. It was 33 years prior to our escape from Earth's destruction!

I feel the effects of the poison now very strongly. It's been only ten minutes since I declared the day a free day and let the younger Turner and the rest of the lab workers off for the day. I'll be dead before I, I mean the younger Turner, arrives at my door and supposes that his coordinator is sleeping just as I did 33 years ago.

I wish Sara were by my side now. Even without her full memory she has been a loving wife these past years. I'm still glad I kept our journey and its cyclical outcome a...a secret...

After a couple of knocks on the coordinator's office door Turner says, "I don't blame him. A rest break and some sleep will be good medicine for him. He has clearly outworked all of us these past few weeks."

DISPATCHER

It's hard to believe that at one time, a very long time ago, I was quite content to live in this place. The temperature is extreme, but the most difficult parts to deal with are the screams and moans outside this office. Most of these people would not be here if my boss had stayed out of their lives. There's where I come in. My job is simple. I'm sent out to negatively affect a person's life to such a degree that they lose all hope for a better life and damn themselves by their reactions before they know what has hit them.

I'm not sure how long I can continue to modify my orders. It's easy enough to outsmart those who have followed me trying to catch me red-handed, so to speak; but I refuse to follow those orders. If I went through with them as ordered, too many lives would be destroyed solely due to my actions.

"Dispatcher, I have completed your next list of orders. In the past, you have had some shaky excuses about why your assignments have not been completed as planned by this office. This is your last chance. If you fail to complete these orders, you will be transferred back to this location. This would be a permanent transfer with no appeal. Do you understand? Of course you do. One of the reasons you were picked for this duty was your intelligence. Understand this, you will be thrown in with all the other residents here if you fail this assignment."

"I understand. May I go now?"

"You may go, but do not even consider playing games with me. I have many spies and some of them will be watching you very closely."

"Yes, I know. With your leave, my lord Satan."

I've seen some of his spies. A bunch of sub-demons that aren't sure which way is up. All I want to do now is get out of here. I'll go back to my apartment in New York and relax a while before looking at this new list.

It was that day on Skull Mountain. Many of the locals called it Golgotha Hill, which was the day that my outlook changed. That day was on my list. I just couldn't bring myself to commit such evil ever again. I cried for months and I ran even longer from the memory before I got the idea of how I could try to make up for all the evil I had perpetrated over the years.

I decided I could continue to take my assignment lists from the boss as I had for centuries. But instead of following them to the letter, I would devise a way for the people I encountered to escape the evil the list contained. Each situation was different and each improvisation was equally as unusual. Like the time when Hitler was on his way to the airport with his top advisors in an automobile caravan.

"Mine Fuhrer, we should be at the airport within the hour."

"We had better be. I have waited long enough to cause the world to submit to my reign. This information contains just the right magnitude to generate a global catastrophe greater than this world has ever seen. Germany will move across the planet and take over before any country can recover."

I found the line of cars traveling along the dirt road towards the airport. It was my assignment to protect the Fuhrer's caravan from the Allied forces who were stationed at several points along the route. The scientists the German leader was counting on were at this very moment being assisted out of the country and into Canada by the United States government. Their work towards the Atomic Bomb had progressed to such a point the Fuhrer could finish its development and conquer the world. They would arrive at the airport at the same time as the Fuhrer, as long as his journey remained uninterrupted.

"Driver, you must go faster. The airplane will not wait forever."

"Yes, mine Fuhrer,"

"With this bomb, we can detonate it over the capitol of each of our enemies. That will surely cause them to listen to the words that will come from Germany and the words that will come from their Fuhrer."

With Hitler planning to drop that many bombs all over the Earth, his actions would result in global destruction. I could not let this happen. I had to come up with a plan to stop the Fuhrer while at the same time not be captured by my boss for disobeying an order. I decided to find the spies that were following me. The same spies that have followed me for over a hundred years.

Normally, my form was very human, as were the forms of the sub-demons that followed me. I appeared to be a tall brunette with a slight streak of blonde just above my forehead and was embodied in a very attractive female body. This shape enabled me to be accepted in almost any situation and it was the only form that these moron sub-demons knew me by.

My plan was to change into a form most hated by the sub-demons, that of an Angel. They can't stand Angels. In fact, each time they see an Angel their anger rages and they seem to become more stupid than they usually are. When I located the four sub-demons behind a small rock formation on the Fuhrer's path along the dirt road, I transformed into the form of an Angel. To the humans, we were still invisible; but, we could see one another quite clearly.

"Hey Bone." He's the leader of the four sub-demons. The other three have similarly intelligent names. They are Bobble, Dog and Slug. They seemed to very happy about it when they were given these names, so they have never changed them. "Bone, what are you and your goblins doing in Germany? Did you lose your way home?"

"Errr, errr." They were never able to talk. They just made grunts and growls.

"Come get me you fools, if you can?"

At that point, I ran down towards the road with the four sub-lives following close behind. Sub-demons, in their human form, are quite squatty looking. They're no more than five feet tall, poorly coordinated, but with the strength of ten humans each. I was trying to capitalize on this combination of characteristics.

They were following very close; as close as I would let them, I was hoping they would be so close they could not watch where they were going if all they could see in front of them was me. I turned to look back at them to see they were all drooling and Bone was grinning like a cat about to catch a mouse. They thought today would be the day they would catch an Angel.

"Pat attention to me boys. I wouldn't want you to lose sight of me."

"Roarrr."

I just love these guys; they're great fun at parties as well. I was almost at my destination with the four of them right behind me. Of course, no one in the caravan could see any of us. We were physically there, but still invisible.

With one sharp upward pull, I shot into the air. Just as I had hoped, those short little misfits couldn't react that quickly. With the force of four rushing torpedoes, they each hit one of the four cars traveling in the Fuhrer's caravan. The impact of the charging, muscular numbskulls, was enough to force the lead car to collide with the others causing the cars to tumble over onto their tops.

The cars would go no further today. The impact also left the four little mounds of demonic ignorance scattered unconscious along the dirt road. I stood at the top of the hillside that overlooked the entire scene and laughed. Not only was I able to stop the Fuhrer from his mission, I had once again outsmarted Bone, Bobble, Dog and Slug.

As the years went by, it had become more and more difficult to sabotage my orders. I could always rely on the ineptitude of my co-workers. There was this once though I had to rely on someone far greater than me.

It was an assignment like any other. I had been given a new list or orders and the first on the list was for me to pose as a baby sitter for a ten-year-old girl. She was a cute little thing who had never hurt a soul. She was on my list because her mother and father were about to get a divorce. Not only that, but her mother and father had been arguing for some time about all kinds of things; so much so, they had said more than once the only reason they were still together was because of the little girl.

The mother and father both worked and were in the habit of taking the little girl to their sitter's house they had used for years. This morning though, they had received a call from the sitter saying she had fallen down and possibly broken her leg so she could not sit for the girl today. My boss is very thorough.

Anyway, I had placed my telephone number on the neighborhood information board at the local grocery store and the girl's mother had found the number. I arrived at their apartment located on the sixteenth floor of an inner-city high rise.

"Hello. You called me as a replacement sitter for the day."

"Yes, come in. There's plenty of food in the refrigerator. Kelly has plenty of games in her room she plays with and any of her friends are welcome to come over if they call. I wish I didn't have to rush off like this; but, I'm already late for work as it is. Kelly, dear, I'm leaving."

Little Kelly came walking slowly from her room balancing herself on her crutches, with both legs in metal braces. She had practically no control over her legs since birth and would more than likely never recover. "You have a good day Mama. I'll be fine."

"You just be yourself and I'll be very proud of you baby."

"We'll be fine Mrs. Johnson. Don't worry about us." I was worried enough for the both of us. I had just finished a meeting with my boss and he was not sympathetic at all with my reasons for failing on my recent assignments. He told me he was losing his patience with me all together. Patience had never been one of his vices.

Kelly's mother left for work and my day with the little girl began. We played games, talked and watched TV for a while before it was time for her afternoon nap. I had dreaded this naptime since the moment I had received my new orders. It was during this nap I was to set fire to the apartment so this lovely little girl would have no chance to escape.

Before she went to sleep, I sat with her for a minute to talk.

"You're a very sweet little girl Kelly."

"Thank you Miss Dee. I like you too."

"Kelly, do you believe in God?"

"Oh yes. I say my prayers every night asking for God to do something to help my mother and father fall in love again so they can be happy together."

"Do you ever ask God to help you?"

"Not often. I don't believe God is hard of hearing. So, if I have asked Him once to fix my legs then I am sure he has heard me."

"I'm sure that's very true Kelly, but will you do me a favor this one time?"

"Sure. What's the favor?"

"Will you say your prayers before your nap and ask God again to heal your legs?"

"Sure. I never get tired of talking to God. Can I ask God to bless you also Miss Dee?"

This was the most beautiful soul I had ever met. "Of course, and thank you dear."

Kelly knelt down at the side of her little bed and silently prayed. The only word she said out loud was "Amen" at the end of her prayer.

"There's a good little girl. Now you lay down and think about your prayer while you are falling to sleep."

I walked away from the little girl feeling so helpless. Demons had long ago lost the right to pray to God, so all I could do was hope. I sat in the living room for over an hour before I caused the furnace to break apart at the seams and engulf the surrounding closet area in flames. I had treated the carpet that went from the edge of the little girl's bed to the front door of the apartment with water just in case she awoke from the smoke and might then be able to escape.

I now sat in the comer of the bedroom looking at the little girl while I cried. I was ordered to stay until, well, until it was over to make sure I didn't mess this one up. The flames were all over the apartment now and there wasn't much hope of this cute little girl waking up. Even if she did, with her crippled legs, she would still be trapped.

Without warning, a blue-white glow came into the girl's room and surrounded her bed. I had never seen anything like it before. The color was so soft it appeared to be full of peace and enriched with love. Kelly began to awaken coughing from the smoke. She saw the flames and jumped from her bed with the legs of an athlete. She paused and looked at her legs while moving her hands slowly down them feeling their strength.

"Miss Dee! Miss Dee! The apartment is on fire!"

She could not see me. I had been invisible in the comer of her room and was all too surprised by the vision I saw to make myself visible.

"I hope she is already out of the building! I've got to get out of here!"

With these words, Kelly ran across the water soaked floor and from the blazing apartment into the hallway and down the steps to the street. As Kelly came running from the front entrance of the apartment building, she saw her mother and father being prevented by the firemen from entering the burning building to save their little girl.

"Mama! Daddy! I'm all right! Look, my legs are healed! I can run!"

I looked down into the street from the window of the burning apartment to see the three of them hugging more strongly than they ever had. I was still crying, but these were tears of happiness. That's when I heard a strange noise coming from the little girl's now engulfed room. To this day, I'm sure I heard, "Thank you Dispatcher."

What an existence this has been. So many assignments are given each day to so many demons like myself. I've been able to disobey orders for a long time, but I'm not sure how long I'll be able to keep it up. When I'm discovered and captured, I'll be thrown into the pit for eternity. I've known that from the start though. I believe what I am doing is more important than what my eternal existence will be.

There was a man that I had shared my secret with during the Civil War. He was a good man who served as a Bishop of the United Brethren in Christ church for nearly fifty years. He was a young man when I first met him. Just married and he and his wife had no children yet, but they planned to when the war was over. He was a very intelligent man who listened to my story and replied very simply this was proof God had and apparently always would work in mysterious ways. I never felt worthy of this assessment. After that, he would speak with me as if I were his friend and not a high-ranking demon.

I would, whenever possible, inform my friend Milton Wright of escaped slaves that were trying to flee to the northern states to find freedom. Milton's church was located in Richmond, Indiana, and was a safe distance from the southern border of Indiana safely allowing those runaway slaves to rest before going further north. At times, Milton and a few of his closest friends would travel to the Kentucky / Indiana state line to personally transport the runaways.

Milton was at the top of my boss's list for years, but each time his name appeared, I was able to protect this good man. He survived the war and became a father to his first son during the year of 1867. His second son was born in 1871. Milton and his wife raised their two sons, Orville and Wilbur, to be kind, inquisitive and innovative.

It was on a morning in the year of 1900 that I received my list of orders from the boss. At the very top of the list were Wilbur and Orville's names, but the names had lines drawn through them.

"Excuse me Sir, but why are these names marked out?"

"It's really none of your business, but it could be a lot of fun for some of you coworkers so I'll tell you. I had originally assigned this project to you but I changed my mind and gave the assignment to Bone, Bobble, Dog and Slug, The look of excitement on their grotesque faces made my day."

"Yes Sir, but what is the assignment?"

"They are to make sure when these two attempt to test their first flight in a manned glider, something goes wrong causing at least one of them to die - preferably Orville since his is currently scheduled to live much longer than his brother. Their father was a great enemy of mine during the Civil War. I was never able to get at him then, but I will get him through his sons."

"I have to be going Sir. I have much work to do if I hope to complete my orders as listed."

"Complete them or you know what the consequence will be!"

I left there as fast as I could and traveled to the place where I was sure to find Wilbur and Orville. Today would be the day they would attempt to glide their small plane down the side of a hill near Kitty Hawk. The name of the hill could not be more gruesome. It was called Kill Devil Hill. Somehow I had to find a way to protect the sons of the only friend I ever had.

I searched for the four sub-demons in order to spy on them with the hope of discovering their plans. They're always easy to find when they are on assignment.

All I had to do is locate the general area and sit and listen. They get so excited on an assignment that they can't stop giggling and howling thinking about how they are going to destroy someone.

I sat near Kill Devil Hill for over an hour listening for their unmistakable noises. At last, I heard them growling just the other side of the hill. I stayed invisible as I gained a vantage to spy on them. They had changed their form to that of geese and were mingling with a gaggle of real geese. When I saw this, their plan became clear to me. They were planning to wait until the flight attempt had commenced and then would lead the geese to fly directly into the path of the glider causing its pilot to lose control and crash.

I needed to stop this. Somehow, I needed to prevent them from being able to guide the geese into the flight path of the glider. I hid and waited until I saw the four growling goons make their move.

They had waited until the twelfth attempt of the two brothers to glide down the mountain because they wanted to kill Orville instead of Wilbur to impressively please their boss. They always were red-nosers with the boss, Orville was at the top of the hill ready to push off while Bone and his goons, looking like geese in the middle of the real gaggle of geese, were waiting on the backside of the hill. Orville pushed off from the top of the hill. Bone stirred up the geese and they began to head straight for the glider's path.

At a point where the geese, real and demonic, were still about fifty feet from the glider, I flew into the sky disguised as my boss and hovered, midair, between the geese and the glider.

"You fools! What do you think you're doing?"

"Ahh? Eerruh?"

My ploy was working. There's something about sub-demons. They must concentrate very hard in order to maintain any form other than their human form. Need I say more? With their concentration broken, they changed back to their human form and began to fall to the ground. This broke up the real geese who flew off in the opposite direction squawking and croaking all the way. Those sub-demons; they fall really well, but they don't land with much style. They hit the earth's surface so hard that they left holes in the ground three feet deep and just lay there stunned, unable to move.

Orville landed without mishap and he and his brother were both very much alive. They were now free to continue their research unencumbered by the gruesome foursome.

I'm thinking back to all of this today because of a most peculiar reason. I'm dying. It's not supposed to be possible for a demon to die since we were created and not born. But it is true. I've been lying in this dark alley for nearly two hours.

A little more than two hours ago my boss sent word for me to meet him here in this alley. He wanted to discuss my success with my current list of orders. When I arrived, it had just gotten dark enough in this alley to make it hard to see for more than fifteen or twenty feet. Then I heard the familiar noises of Bone, Bobble, Dog and Slug. They were walking down the alley towards me almost giggling.

"I thought the boss was to be here boys?"

"I am here Dispatcher. I have been waiting for you."

"What can I do for you Sir?"

"Two things. The first is to stop pretending you really think of me as your lord whose orders you are anxious to follow. The second is to die."

"To die? But I can't die. I'm a demon and demons don't die. They're punished."

"Not this time Dispatcher. This time you will die. After finding out what you have been up to for the past two thousand years, I do not want to hear your name again. So, I will merely cause you to cease to exist."

"Fine! I'd rather not exist than to serve you in any way Satan!"

"The die you shall."

At that moment, Satan motioned to his four fierce fools to move in on me. I no longer had any of my powers. I was helpless to their attacks. They were very thorough.

They beat me in such a way I would die slowly, painfully and alone. It's almost over though. I can feel the last bit of life leaving my battered body.

What's this? I see something moving slowly down the alley towards me. It's the blue-white light I saw in the little girl's bedroom that fiery night. It's hovering over me. So, why do I feel so peaceful and unafraid?

A voice spoke from the glow, "Dispatcher, He knows all you have done. He knows you choose, of your own free will, to not be a slave to sin and torment. He knows you would rather die than carry out any further hardship on mankind. Anyone who dies has been freed from sin. He died once for all of us. In the same way, count yourself dead to sin but alive to God. Sin shall not be you master because you are under God's grace for all of the good you have done since the crucifixion."

At that very moment, I died and was born to a new life.

A life as an Angel.

THE RAPID EYE MURDERS

"Lieutenant, you'd better listen to this." The uniformed officer was standing near the check-in counter of the Hotel Roberts. He was holding a large, bulky cassette recorder and a couple of cassette tapes in his hands.

"I'll be there in a minute. Whatever you have there can wait." The Lieutenant had just began to question the hotel's night auditor. It was the night auditor that found the third body. It seems that the magnetic lock to the room of the third murder victim found in the Muncie Hotel in as many days had malfunctioned and the housekeeper could not get in to clean the room. When the housekeeper brought the night auditor to the room, they unlocked the door together. "I need to make sure they haven't disturbed the latest victim's room any more than it already has been. The last two were a mess."

"Lieutenant, I think you're gonna want to listen to this before you go any further with them." The uniform was determined.

"Will you excuse me? It seems that my plan, the investigation plan of the Detective in charge of this case," he said with rude sarcasm, "needs to succumb to the wishes of the uniformed officer over there." The Lieutenant pointed loosely towards the reservation desk. With no response from the hotel staff to the Lieutenant comments, the Lieutenant continued his verbal bashing as he slowly turned and walked towards the uniformed officer. "Yes, that's the one. The one who graduated from the academy just this past fall."

The uniformed officer slightly dipped his eyes below those of the Lieutenant as they came closer to one another. A reaction that both pleased and angered the Lieutenant.

"Listen boy," began the surly Lieutenant, "If what you have is so important for me to leave what I'm doing to answer to your beckon call, then don't dip your head like a cowardly lamb."

The uniformed officer raised his head and slowly forced his shoulders back. As he did, the Lieutenant continued, "But this better be good kid. I don't like to be interrupted, ever; by anyone. Especially by a pup who's barely house trained."

The uniformed officer spoke slowly with clear and methodic meter. "The desk clerk said that the victim brought this recorder with these two tapes to the desk last night around 9:00pm. He left instructions for them to be returned to him when he checked out."

The Lieutenant interrupted with a quick and dry delivery, "So the desk clerk figures that since our victim has checked out, even though he still hasn't left the building, that these tapes should be placed with the rest of his personal belongings." The volume in the Lieutenant's voice began to grow with every syllable, "I, for the life of me, do not believe that I was pulled from questioning those two over there to help you sort out the dead man's luggage."

"Lieutenant," the uniformed officer said with a more forceful voice than he had used before, "There was more to the victim's message."

"Oh please," questioned the Lieutenant, "do tell. Are we to carry his dry cleaning to the hearse alongside the body when the coroner brings it down?"

"No sir." The officer was again sheepish. "The rest of the message only says 'notes of my investigations' on side A of tapes one and two. It's the side B message that I believe you will find interesting."

"Well son," barked the Lieutenant. "I'm over here and I'm listening."

The uniformed officer spoke firmly, yet nearly in a whisper, as he read the message from the B-side of tape two. "The message on side B reads, 'Revelations about the killer."

The Lieutenant was uncomfortably quiet. He took the tape from the officer and saw the tiny scribbling on side B of tape two. The Lieutenant looked and found no such note on the B-side of tape one.

"Well now," growling in his usual tone, "how long were you going to let me stand over there before you told me about these tapes? Grab that recorder and let's you and I go somewhere and see what we have on these tapes."

The Lieutenant kept the tapes and the uniformed officer brought the recorder as they stepped into one of the side meeting rooms. With the doors closed and the room empty except for the two of them, the Lieutenant placed tape two in the recorder with side B queued to play.

"It's only static sir," complained the officer with a hint of surprise in his voice.

"That it is. But from the scratchy sound of it, I've got a hunch that this tape has been erased." The Lieutenant continued as he took the tape from the player, flipped it to queue up side A, "My gut tells me that the killer watched as last night's victim delivered these tapes to the front desk. Our killer's been here all the time. One of the guests or employees of the hotel. If the message on side A is correct and last night's dead man was investigating the murders on his own, then my hunch is that our killer erased the tape and proceeded to kill the amateur Sherlock before he exposed the truth."

Obviously startling them both, a voice began to emerge from the tape player from side A, the side marked "notes of my investigations.[5] The Lieutenant stopped the tape. "Why would our killer not erase both sides? For that matter, why'd the killer leave the tapes in the first place? They could have been taken a lot more easily than taking the time to erase even one side. Unless the killer erased tape two's B-side before they were delivered to the front desk."

The two of them sat silently for a moment. Then the Lieutenant spoke first, "I tell you what junior. The coroner's office will be a while in number three's room. So in the meantime, you and I are going to listen to Sherlock's taped investigation notes here and see what he thinks he found. More importantly, I want to hear why the killer didn't mind us or anyone else getting these two tapes but did not want us to hear whatever was on that missing side B."

The Lieutenant queued up tape one, side A. The voice from the third victim spoke from the cassette player.

As the tape began, a male voice started pouring from the inefficient speaker. "It's Thursday, around 9:00am. My name is William Burke, Bill. I'm starting this tape to record my thoughts concerning the murder last evening of a friend of mine. Her name was Janus Solon. Like me, Janus was a writer. The truth of the matter is that this Hotel is filled with writers. A mid-west gathering of nearly two hundred writers are here networking and continuing to learn how we might get our written efforts published.

"Janus was about 35. She had found some success with her writing but the brass ring was still just out of reach. They found her this morning when her wakeup call had gone unanswered.

"My room is on the same floor and I noticed the commotion in the hall. I ventured down the hall to her open door. Walking into the room, all seemed quite normal. The bed was made. Clothes were hanging in the closet alcove. Two pair of shoes were neatly placed beneath the hanging clothes; one pair of dress shoes and a pair of casual.

"There was a casual outfit of khaki shorts with a flowery pale-blue pull-over Henley lying next to it. The knit socks draped over one leg of the khakis were matched with the Henley. Walking further into the room I noticed the bathroom door slightly ajar. I moved slowly in that direction and stood alone for a moment at the bathroom doorway.

"The first thing to catch my eye was the peculiar mixture of red and mint green on the mirror at eye level. A split second later I lowered my eyes and saw Janus's body slumped over the bathroom sink. She was fully covered with an emerald green, terry cloth bathrobe. Her arms were weakly clinging to the vanity from beneath her shoulders to her outstretched hands. Her toothbrush still rested in her right hand.

There was a large, brick red matting of hair on the crown of Janus's skull. It appeared she had been struck from behind while she was brushing her teeth. The splattering on the mirror in front of her was a mixture of blood and toothpaste.

"No one was in the bathroom with the body when I stepped in. That's when I noticed the blood covered portable printer on the floor at Janus's feet. It sat in a small pool of blood that had drizzled down from what appeared to be the impact point of the printer's sharp, rear corner. There was still a small, tom piece of paper hanging from the printer's spool.

"I looked around the small bathroom and saw nothing else that caught my eye until I saw Janus's frightened eyes reflecting back at me in the mirror. Her chin rested on the front edge of the vanity with her mouth slightly open as if she were trying to say something. Maybe to say who she saw in the mirror her murderer.

"That's when I saw the paper. A small comer of the paper was protruding from Janus's mouth. Contrary to all I had learned many years before about not touching elements of a crime scene, I reached into Janus's mouth and pulled out the paper. It took a little tugging at first, then it finally released. It was a torn piece of 8 1/2 ´ 11 paper that appeared to match up to the remaining piece still held by the printer. It seemed she had been struck from behind with the printer and then this piece of paper was shoved deep and firm into her throat.

"Janus did not die from the blow to the head, but rather from suffocation caused by the torn writing paper blocking her airway. Not a pleasant death to say the least.

Following my retrieving the paper from Janus's now still throat, I heard some movement from others in the bed area and moved quickly out of the room and back to my own."

Side one of tape one went silent.

"Lieutenant, I heard nothing about any paper found in the first victim's mouth in our reports."

"That's because we did not discover the paper. If Sherlock here is telling the truth, then he tampered with the crime scene and has withheld evidence. I want you to go to the phone and call the forensics lab. Tell them to search the throat of Janus Solon for any foreign materials especially any remnants of paper.

"I'll stay here and begin to listen to this second tape from our boy Billy Burke, victim number three." The Lieutenant thought for a moment as the uniformed officer stood and began to leave the room to carry out his command. "Hey, pup."

"Yes Sir?" The uniform stopped in his tracks.

"While you're at it, I want a rundown William Burke. I'd like to know what gave him the idea to go Sherlock on everybody. Who knows, maybe he wrote about murders."

With those last words, the uniformed officer left the room.

"OK Sherlock. Let's see what you have for us on tape two."

Side A of tape two began much the same as tape one had.

"It's Friday morning just after 10:00am. My name is Bill Burke and these are the notes of my investigation of the murder of a second of my friends here at the Hotel Roberts. Last night, now appears to be a serial process continued. I had returned to my room during a break following our first workshop.

I saw the Hotel manager pull the room door nearly closed and speak to a sobbing member of his staff 'I want you to go and get yourself something to drink. I'll call the police from my office I do not want to disturb the room any more than I have. That Lieutenant nearly killed me for having my staff call the police from room. I won't do that again."

"With that, the hallway cleared except for me. I walked towards the room door. It was still slightly ajar. It was Alene's room. I felt an eerie feeling as I gently pushed the door open and entered the room. Alene Seraph had been a member of the local writer's group I had attended since my early retirement, just as Janus had been. We, as well as others, had decided to attend this Muncie workshop in hopes of igniting our writing careers. For Janus and Alene that hope had cost them their lives.

"I stepped calmly into the room and took a quick look around. The sight was most disturbing. Lying on the bed was Alene. She was positioned on her back with the thermo-blanket neatly pulled over her pajama-draped chest. Her arms were on top of the blanket stretched out to her sides. Both hands were still desperately grasping the blanket as if she were trying to free herself from the clutches of death itself.

"Alene's eyes were staring straight up from her now motionless body. As I moved closer, I saw her swollen, beaten temples. Both sides of her head looked as if they had been powerfully struck. Next to Alene's head, on the pillow to the right of her, rested a bloodied laptop computer. It was closed and looked to be a very effective weapon.

"It was then I noticed the indentations on the bed. I looked closely at the pressure indentations on either side of Alene's body. They were even with her waist. I saw that Alene's arms were both bruised. The bruises were near the inside of her elbows and directly in line with the indentations on the bed.

"It seems the killer sat on top of Alene and her thermo-blanket, directly astride her waist with their brutal knees holding her arms down preventing her from struggling free.

"I looked at Alene's face and eyes. I saw the fear of struggle. Her skin had a slight blue tint to it and her mouth was open. There it was again. I gently grasped the end of the paper and pulled it free from the depth of her throat. It was pieces of crumpled, bloody newspaper.

"Alene, like Janus, had not died from her most obvious injuries. She had both died from suffocation as a result of the paper being jammed so deeply into her throat. But why? Alene more than likely would have died from the direct blows to her head. She fought for her last breath of air while the killer sat astride her, cruelly pinning her arms to the bed while stuffing the newspaper down her dying throat."

Tape two went silent.

The Lieutenant was beside himself. "What is it with this guy? He goes onto two fresh crime scenes where he shouldn't be in the first place. He tampers with and then takes vital evidence from those crime scenes only to record his observations and then admits on tape that he took the evidence. And now he's dead himself. Well, it's clear to me that if the killer knew our 'Sherlock' Burke had taken the papers from the mouths of the killer's first two victims, then Burke's days were certainly numbered. Either the killer would be concerned that Burke would discover his identity or would be really ticked off for messing with his masterpieces."

"Lieutenant," the uniformed officer spoke as if he were out of breath as he re-entered the room. "I called Forensics. They had already found traces of what appears to be paper deep in the first victim's throat."

"I can tell you now Pup, they'll find paper traces in the second victim's throat as well."

"What Sir? I don't follow you."

"Never mind. What did you find out about Burke? I know he's retired, but from what?"

"He was a cop, Sir."

"What did you say?"

"A Cop, Sir. He had been a Detective in Indianapolis until he retired five years ago to go off and write his novel."

"He's not old enough to fully retire boy. Did he have his twenty in?"

"Barely Sir. He was forced to retire early after he suffered a nervous breakdown. His report claims the pressure of too many unsolved murders finally got to him."

"Murders? Did you say murders?"

"Yes Sir. He was a Homicide Detective."

The Lieutenant stood quickly and headed for the elevator. "Grab the tapes and the recorder Boy. We're going to have a visit with the late Mr. Burke."

The Lieutenant and the uniformed officer arrived at the latest crime scene. There were still forensic staffers everywhere. The hotel room was clogged with moving figures taking pictures and searching the corners of the room for whatever they might consider unusual.

The Lieutenant spoke to the officer at the room's doorway. "What do we have here?"

"Well Sir," replied the Detective Sergeant, another of the Lieutenant's subordinates, "You can have a look for yourself. They're finishing up right now."

They both walked into the room with the uniformed officer at their heels. The Detective Sargent began his report to his Lieutenant. "We found Mr. Burke sitting upright here in this side chair. He was wedged snuggly between the desk and his chair, which is apparently what kept him from falling to the floor. It seems from the preliminary that the victim had ingested a full bottle of prescription sleeping pills sometime after 8:00pm last evening,"

"Based on what evidence?"

"Well Sir, the bottle sitting there on the desk was filled last evening at the pharmacy across the street and they have a record of the sale occurring at 8:00pm. The bottle was filled with 60 tablets. The dosage should have been one tablet."

"Alright Sergeant. Go on."

"Yes Sir. As you can see the victim also has a plastic laundry bag wrapped around his head with the end tied off in the front."

"Any signs of struggle? Any bruises on his arms?"

"No Sir. We've seen no visible bruises or any sign of struggle."

The Lieutenant walked around the room but never took his eyes off Burke's body. Here was 'Sherlock' Burke, sitting in his room at the Hotel Roberts up right in a side chair with enough downers in his system to have killed him two or three times over and a plastic bag tied around his head for good measure.

"Things are different here." The Lieutenant was speaking to no one and no one was paying any attention. "No blunt blow to the head. Pills instead. No blood anywhere. The eyes are closed. No sign of struggle. This guy went too easy."

It was then that the Lieutenant saw it. "Has the body been dusted and all of the photos taken?" The Lieutenant posed the question to the Detective Sargent who did not quickly respond. The Lieutenant then barked, "Well have they?"

"Yes Sir. They're done with the body."

With that, the Lieutenant took the plastic from Burke's head. Pulling a new bag from his inside blazer pocket and a pair of tweezers from his shirt pocket, the Lieutenant reached in the mouth of the dead Burke and recovered what appeared to be misplaced evidence.

"Sargent, note that I am pulling two pieces of paper from the victim's mouth. A piece of plain stationary covered with what appears to be blood and toothpaste and a piece of crumpled newspaper."

The uniformed officer then sheepishly interrupted, "Lieutenant, you'd better listen to this."

"You again, Pup. What have you found this time?" The Lieutenant looked up as the officer brought over a cassette tape labeled 'tape 3.' "What's it say Boy?"

"Side A reads, 'notes of my investigations."

"Here we go again. OK. I'll bite. What is written on side B?"

The officer read side B to the Lieutenant. "Side B reads, 'Why Burke had to die."

The Lieutenant didn't even flinch. The officer was nearly bouncing. The Lieutenant then said calmly, "Well son, did you bring the recorder like I told you to?"

"Yes Sir."

"Then let's have a listen to this third, and apparently final tape in the Sherlock Burke series."

The A-side of tape three began to play.

"My name is Bill Burke. I've been considering the aspects of the murders of two of my friends during the past two days. I've pondered on the facts of these murders and I have come to only one clear conclusion. I'm next."

The tape went silent.

"Well son, let's hear the other side of this tape to see if it lives up to its name."

Now the B-side of tape three began to play. The side labeled, 'Why Burke had to die.'

"All I wanted to do was write."

"Sir!"

"I know Pup. It's Burke's voice. Let's listen."

"After they kicked me off of IPD, I wanted to write fiction so I could create a world where I could control the outcome. It went quite well for the first two years. I finished my first novel and started working on my second. But that's when the trouble started. No one wanted to publish my work.

"They didn't seem to understand all of the pain, sweat and tears that go into a novel. "No thanks' is all I would hear or read. I began to have a lot of trouble sleeping, so a doctor prescribed some sleeping pills. They worked right from the start. I slept all through the night.

"And that's when the wild dreams started as well. I dreamed of things in my dreams I had never dreamed about before. And they were so real and vivid. I really enjoyed them, for the most part, until this past week.

"I started dreaming about the writer's workshop here in Muncie. I thought about all of the writers that would be attending trying to get some attention for their writing. I thought about the pain they felt; the heartache they must experience from the constant effort and the constant rejection. I started dreaming about killing them to release them from their pain on the first night of the conference.

"I dreamed that I had killed Janus. She wrote very well and seemed to enjoy reading her works to other writers. But other writers were the only ones listening. So I dreamed that I used an old magnet trick I had learned to introduce a magnetic charge to the key card to my room, and placed it into the magnetic door lock to Janus's room. It worked like it always did in the past.

"She was going to go down to the bar later. Her outfit was neatly laid out on the bed. I knew she was only planning to drown the pain. As I stepped through her room, I saw the printer that had been giving her such trouble recently. I disconnected it from the laptop and walked around to the entrance to the bathroom. I saw her in my dream. She was leaning over the sink brushing her teeth. I came up behind her and as she raised her head mid saw me in the mirror, I swung the printer hard against the back of her head.

"It was so real, even though it was just a dream. Janus collapsed straight to her knees with her arms and chin still on the vanity. She was still alive, in my dream, so I ripped the paper from the printer and shoved it down her throat. I had to hold onto her, in my dream, to keep her from falling to the floor during her struggle to cough the paper from her throat.

"That's all of the dream that I remembered from that night. The next day, I discovered she had been killed just as I had dreamed. I took the paper from her mouth. I knew it would lead me to her killer.

"Then, on Thursday evening, I dreamed that I entered Alene's room while she was asleep. Alene was a good person; an Angel to a fault. Her pain had to be unbearable with all of the rejections from agents and publishers. I dreamed that I took her laptop from the small desk in her room and hit her hard on the side of the head. She jerked her head up from the bed, in my dream, so I had to hit her on the other side of her head as I swung back around.

"In my dream, I tucked her back in bed. I knew she had written for newspapers in the past, so I hovered above her, in my dream, and held her down as I shoved the newspaper down her throat. She finally stopped fighting and accepted the peace of mind I was giving her, in my dream.

"But then on Friday, when I saw her lying in her bed, I took the paper from her mouth because I felt sure it would lead me to the killer. I felt that whoever had killed my two friends would now be after me.

"I felt tired and believed that only with a good night's sleep, would I be able to dream these fears away. I had my prescription filled, gave the tapes to the front desk to help in the investigation in case I was next, and went to my room.

"I could only sleep for short periods. I took more pills each time I awoke to help me get back to sleep. I was very tired, nodding off a little here and there, but not fully asleep. I dreamed that I recorded a tape, this tape in fact, during one of my naps. And then I had the really bad dream.

"I am sure, from what I saw in my dream, that I will need to pretend to be dead because the killer is after me. I placed the two pieces of paper I still have in my pocket into my mouth. After placing the stationary and newspaper into my mouth, I will loosely place a plastic bag over my head and pretend to be dead."

The tape ended.

The Lieutenant stood sadly shaking his head, "Now don't that just beat all."

"Well, Pup, looks like we're done here. Our Sherlock Burke is one writer who has gotten his last rejection notice."

THE END

THE COFFEE TABLE

When you're ten years old, a lot of things seem to matter. Learning your multiplication tables, what your friends are doing after school, why it is that girls are starting to look better than they used to, and sometimes the painful reality that your allowance just doesn't go very far. I remember being ten. In fact, I remember a lot about that year. But one thing always seems to stand out over the rest. My Mom's birthday.

When I realized that it was only two months away, my allowance looked smaller than it ever had. And to make matters worse, Mom had been saying for nearly a year that she wanted a new coffee table for our living room. Dad didn't seem to be listening to Mom. Whenever Mom would mention it, Dad just stayed silent. Don't get me wrong, Dad and Mom were very much in love. The problem seemed to be that Dad just wasn't getting the hint.

I thought about asking for a raise in my allowance if I agreed to do some extra things around the house. I was sure I could find enough to do during the next two months to raise enough to buy a coffee table. I mean, they couldn't cost much more than twenty dollars. They weren't that big. But if I asked for more allowance, Mom would want to know why. One thing I had discovered early on was that I couldn't lie very well to Mom. She always saw right through me. And besides, asking Mom for more money for me to buy her a gift was like asking Mom to go buy her own gift. I needed another alternative.

About halfway between home and school was a furniture store. It was located on the comer of the only busy intersection I had to cross to get to school. I would stand on the sidewalk at that comer waiting for the stoplight to change green and never paid much attention to the fact that it was a furniture store. Now was different though. Mom wanted a coffee table.

In the morning, on my way to school, the store was closed. So, on my way home one afternoon, I decided to go inside the store to have a look around. It only took a moment for me to find the small section of coffee tables that were on display. Wow, here they were. Six to choose from, if I only had the money.

"Can I help you son?"

The question startled me at first. I hadn't seen anyone else in the store. "My Mom wants a coffee table for her birthday."

"When's her birthday? Is it soon?"

"It's in two months. It's just a week before mine, but she's a lot older than I am." I knew the moment I said the words how stupid it sounded.

"Is that a fact?" The man didn't laugh at me or make any comment about my ridiculous statement about my Mom being older than me. "Do you have a gift in mind for her?"

"She wants a coffee table. Which of these" as I pointed to the six tables in front of us "is the closest to twenty dollars."

"Is that how much you have to spend?"

"Well, I don't have the money yet. But I plan to do some extra work to earn the twenty dollars before her birthday."

"How about a nice lamp? Would she like a lamp?"

"No. We have lamps all over the house. Besides, I think she has her heart set on a coffee table."

"I'm sorry young man, but each of these tables sell for eighty dollars." I'm sure my face contorted to a look the man hadn't expected. "Are you alright son?"

"Eighty dollars! There's no way I could get eighty dollars." I turned and slowly started walking out of the store. "Thank you sir. I need to leave now."

Just as I got to the door ready to walk out, the man spoke. "Young man, wait a minute. My name is Mr. Sherman. What's your name?"

"Russ, sir. It's short for Russell."

He looked me in the eye for what seemed to be a long time before he spoke again "Getting your Mom a coffee table is really important to you isn't it?"

"She's been talking about wanting one for about a year. But I can't find eighty dollars in two months. It would take me until her next birthday to make that kind of money."

"Would you like to work for me here at the store? After school of course."

"Thank you, but I'm only ten years old."

"If I spoke with your dad and he agreed, would you be interested?"

"Sure! But I only have two months before her birthday. I can't make that kind of money even with a real job."

You're right son, so here's my offer. I'll sell you the coffee table of your choice for what it cost me to buy. Then you can come here after school and work until about five o'clock each afternoon until your Mom's birthday. Instead of me paying you any money, I'll apply it towards the cost of the Coffee table. You've got two months before you need it. I think that will work out just fine. What do you think about that deal?"

I remember thinking, a real job and I can get Mom's table.' I walked over to Mr. Sherman and put out my hand. "You've got a deal, Sir."

"Good. Why don't you ask your dad to come in to see me tomorrow and we'll make our plan."

The next day my dad met with Mr. Sherman. I stood near the coffee tables while they talked.

"Russ."

"Yes Dad?"

"Come on over here for a minute."

I joined them around a desk where Mr. Sherman had his papers spread out. "Yes Sir?"

Mr. Sherman and I have talked and if you want to work for him for the next two months after school, it's fine with me."

"Thanks Dad. Yes I do want to." I turned my head back to look where the coffee tables were. "Can I pick one out today?"

They both laughed a little and then Mr. Sherman spoke, "Of course Russ. Let's go pick."

I started my new job the very next day. It was a Wednesday and I had originally planned to go to the movies with a group of my friends. I firmly told them that I couldn't go. I had to go to work.

They were impressed and I was filled with pride.

When I arrived at about 3:30 that afternoon, Mr. Sherman greeted me at the door. "Hello young man. Ready to get started?"

I nodded yes and my new job began. I spent many of the afternoons with the same assignments. First, I would take a dry dust cloth and start at the front of the store. I was to dust off all of the furniture until I had worked my way to the back. When I had finished with that project, Mr. Sherman would have a cold can of Coke waiting for me at the rear of the store. "You're doing a good job Russ. Keep it up."

When I had finished my Coke, I would return to the front of the store. This time my assignment was to sweep the floor. The store had a tile floor throughout, except in the very back of the store where the tile was missing and the concrete floor beneath the tile was visible. Mr. Sherman said that I should sweep slowly. That way, I wouldn't throw any of the dust from the floor back up on the furniture. When I had finished the floor, on most days, I was done for the day, I usually finished around five o'clock as we had agreed and headed on home.

I had been working for Mr. Sherman for nearly a month and all was going well. I completed the same assignments each day, Monday through Friday, with Mr. Sherman sitting with me when I had finished with the furniture dusting and having a Coke. There was one day that was a bit different.

I had just finished with the dusting and wound up in the back of the store as always. Mr. Sherman wasn't back there though. I turned to look around the store and he was talking with a man about some furniture for the man's living room. Mr. Sherman saw me look over to him and he gave me a big smile in return. It looked like I would be having my Coke alone today.

The Cokes were kept in the very back of the store in a medium sized, white refrigerator. As I walked towards it to find my Coke, I noticed that there was a big dirty smear around the handle. My job was to clean, so I turned and went for one of my cloths.

The dry cloth wasn't budging the dirt no matter how hard I tried. I rubbed and rubbed on the refrigerator door to no avail. I decided I needed some soap and water so I took my cloth to the bathroom and got it good and wet in the hand-washing sink. I put some of the hand soap on the cloth by rubbing the bar of Dial on the cloth a few times.

As I left the bathroom to return to my effort with the dirty refrigerator, I could see that Mr. Sherman was still with the same man looking at the same living room furniture. I went on about my task of trying to clean the dirty refrigerator door before I would sit to have my Coke.

As I touched the wet, soapy cloth to the dirty handle area on the refrigerator door, I immediately noticed the dirt started coming off. A split second later, I felt hot and tingly all over. The hand I was washing the door with stopped moving and was frozen in front of me still against the refrigerator door. I felt like my body began to hop, but now my whole body was stiff.

I couldn't force the word "Ouch" out of my mouth. All I could muster was "AAAHHH" before the lights went out.

When the lights began coming back on, I was laying on one of the new sofas near the back of the furniture show room. Mr. Sherman and my dad were both leaning over me and saying my name. All I could think of was that Mr. Sherman had called my dad. He had called my dad! I must have broken the refrigerator.

I opened my eyes as far as I could but I still couldn't see very well. "Mr. Sherman?" "Russ. What is it boy?" He sounded eager.

"I'm sorry I broke your refrigerator." I licked my lips and continued. "Can I still get the coffee table for my Mom?"

"Son," my dad spoke up. "You didn't break the refrigerator."

"I didn't? Oh, good."

With a small laugh in his voice, Mr. Sherman spoke. "Of course you can still get the coffee table. In fact, why don't you take the rest of this week off from work? You can come in again on Monday; work a couple of days next week and that should be enough for you to get your mom's coffee table. If that's alright with your dad?"

"That sounds good to me. Dad, is it alright with you?"

My father looked deep into my eyes. One of the deepest looks I ever remember sharing with him. "On one condition. Don't try to clean that refrigerator again; deal?"

"You bet," I replied with a slight relief in my voice. "I think that refrigerator bit me."

My Mom had that coffee table in her living room for over twenty years. I think she liked it. In fact, I think she liked it a lot.

UNTIL DEATH DO US PART

I stepped to the front porch just as I had for the past five years. Each day coming home looking forward to hearing my wife's voice calling to me from some distant part of our large two-story colonial. We were in love. My coming home was the beginning of a new evening of talking and touching; of sharing the experiences of the day; of cuddling one another into a night of pleasant dreams. My footsteps had not sounded on the wooden porch for more than a month. Not since the divorce.

With the key poised to enter the slot, I could not put aside the hopes that it had all been a nightmare. It had started with the letters. Return addresses missing and covered with the strong fragrance of exotic perfume. Each envelope had been placed into our roadside mailbox addressed only to "My Darling Russell."

I found the first two and kept them to myself, burning them in the fireplace; but that did not erase the memory of their content. Endless pleas to turn my heart from my wife and cast my attentions to the anonymous sender. They were never signed. Each note ended the same way. "Until death do us part."

My wife Barbara found the next five notes. It seemed she understood the notes were a prank or a demented attempt to cause a problem where no problem existed.

We were fine until the telephone calls started. The woman on the line never spoke her name but pledged her undying love and her willingness to do whatever it would take to make it possible for us to be together. Barbara interrupted on the last call telling the woman to leave us alone. The woman calmly told Barbara that she held no ill feelings toward her but that she would never give me up. She said that I was the difference between life and death for her. It was her eerie, determined voice that drove Barbara away.

Barbara left a week ago. She said she didn't want the house. She took a few of the things we had once called ours, and left. In a way I don't blame her, but since I had not broken our commitment to have and to hold, I still felt cheated.

The door opened and I reached to place my keys on the middle shelf of the narrow, upright gun cabinet as I had for years. The cabinet was for umbrellas with the exception of the only handgun I had ever owned. The standard action 9mm Beretta was kept in the small, inside drawer at the top of the closed cabinet. Barbara was not a fan of guns. But the Beretta had never been an issue. As I placed my keys on the shelf, I noticed that the handgun drawer was slightly open. I reached my hand up to the drawer and closed it without another thought.

It was then I heard the voice. "Darling, I'll be down in a minute."

The voice came from somewhere upstairs. I walked cautiously from the kitchen back towards the front door. I leaned my upper body over the railing as I looked up the stair well. I saw no movement. I began to walk up the stairs when I heard, "I found my favorite dress today. It's something I haven't worn for a very long time. I wanted tonight to be special with it being your first night back home."

My eyes were now just high enough to see down the hallway of the second floor. I looked and saw that the door to the master bedroom was open.

And then I saw her. From behind, she was strikingly attractive. The curves of her body flowed beneath the enticing cut of her evening gown. As she turned, still not aware I was watching, I studied her profile. Long, athletic legs stretching elegantly from her black high-heeled shoes up through the shear, black lace gown that tightly covered her trim, well-balanced figure and ending by barely covering her perfectly poised breasts.

My eyes moved up her neckline to the left side of her face in absolute horror. The woman in my bedroom was not Barbara and the woman in my bedroom had a hideous skeletal face with only a hint of thin white hair grossly scattered on her head. She turned and saw me, "My darling Russell. Aren't you the impatient one. I'll be right down."

I nearly fell as I began to rush down the stairs. Before I had reached the first floor. That voice stopped me in my tracks. "Dinner will be ready in another five minutes." This time the voice came from the kitchen. I leaned around from the stairwell to peer down the hall to the kitchen. There she was. The same black gown. The same black high-heeled shoes. The same hideous face.

I stepped slowly from the stairs to the gun cabinet. Opening it, I reached up to the drawer I had closed only a moment before. The Beretta was not there. The drawer was empty.

I turned to bolt for the front door and there she was.

She was standing between me and the door with a smile that sent chills through my shoulders and a blend of fear and anger through my soul.

"Who are you?" I barked.

"My darling, what a question to ask. Come here and let me show you how much I love you." With those words she began a slow walk towards me with her arms reaching to hold me. I turned and moved quickly towards the kitchen.

She was already there.

I was so startled that I stumbled sending us both colliding into the breakfast table and falling to the floor. I fell to my back and she was lying on top of me with her zombie-like face only inches from my own. My hands went immediately to the sides of her face to prevent her from kissing me. Her strength was astounding. It took all of my own strength to keep the distance between our faces at a horrible few inches.

I was applying such pressure to her face during our struggle that I began to see the paper thin tissue tear from the bones of her face. There was no blood; only bones being exposed with no related reaction from the struggling woman.

"My darling Russell, let me love you." She repeated these words over and over throughout the struggle forcing her monstrous skeletal face even closer to my own.

All of my struggling to keep her from kissing me caused us to recklessly move across the kitchen floor away from the foyer hall towards the back door of the house.

"My darling Russell, let me love you."

We continued to struggle as I crashed into the wooden trash bin. My head hit the bin a couple of times causing it to tip and fall. The clumsy trash container first hit my head and then it collided with the grotesque head of the crazed, hideous woman. After striking us both, the wooden bin spilled its contents onto the floor beside our entangled struggle.

The shine of the metal caught my eye.

"My darling Russell, let me love you."

Someone had thrown it into the trash. I removed my right hand from the throat of this viscous monster who was hovering over me. I knew I could only hold her off with just my left hand for a few heartbeats.

"My darling Russell, let me love you."

I reached my right hand into the trash bin and wrapped my exhausted fingers around the grip of the Beretta. I pulled the gun from the bin with no reaction from the skull woman.

I spoke to her for the first time and said, "Your notes said 'until death do us part.'"

"Yes my darling Russell, 'Until death do us part.'"

I placed the gun to the right side of her decaying skull and growled at this hideous beast that had cost my marriage and was now trying to somehow steal my life. "Then die you monstrous Bitch." I feverishly unloaded the entire clip shattering her head into pieces across the kitchen floor.

Her body fell away from mine to the floor next to me. There was no blood from the shattered head or from the headless body.

I got to my knees still shaking from the ordeal. My breathing was quick and shallow. I stood and lumbered towards the front door.

That's when I heard the voice. I turned my head quickly to stare over my shoulder into the kitchen.

There she was.

The headless body of the monster who stalked me even from death.

She was standing upright, walking slowly towards me from the kitchen with her arms raised and reaching out to me. That demonic voice erupted from the headless body pleading, "My darling Russell, let me love you."

THE BROKEN HOUR GLASS

The clock on the wall seems so quiet tonight compared to the way that thing usually clunks almost off the wall. Can't see it too well all the way over there anyway; I'll have Eddie move it closer the next time he visits. Who knows when that will be though? It seems like it's been a month since he's been here. Where's my calendar, I'm sure it was last month. This drawer is such a mess - I can't find anything in here. You'd think for the price these people are being paid around here they'd keep things a little cleaner especially my drawer. Ah, they don't clean my drawer anymore. I guess I got a little mean to a couple of them last time they tried. I don't blame them for keeping their hands out of my stuff as loud as I got when they were in here last. What a bastard I've become since I broke my hip, and everyone is being so nice they never call me that but I see it in their faces. Forget the calendar, I know it was at least a month since Eddie was here last.

"Mr. Sinew, it's time for your dinner. I hope you'll like the hash tonight, it looks really good. I'll just swing your table over your bed here and you can adjust your bed so you're sitting up while I get your tray off of the cart."

"I hope that it's better than it was the last time the cook tried to pass it off as food. I used to have an old German Sheppard that was nothing but trouble, but I never would have tried to feed that garbage to him," She's probably thinking that I'm the old dog... why don't they just say it to my face instead of talking behind my back or even worse, not saying a word - just thinking it to themselves. "This bed is so slow. I've had my finger on this button since you first came in and it's still not all the way up."

"Well Mr. Sinew, I'm in no hurry. What do you say that we both just sit here and wait until this bed of yours is through playing around?"

"Oh, it'll be alright. Just leave my tray and go on with your work. I'm sure you have more important things to do than to sit around with an old, decrepit man whose as tired of this bad food as he is his bad life; life, there's a joke."

"Mr. Sinew, you're just a little grumpy today aren't you? I'll leave you with your dinner and let you relax for a while."

Please just leave me alone. These people have no idea of what's going on here. Can their lives be so fruitful that they have no time for depression, no time for sadness, or no time for the cold reality of dying a little every day? I've lived eighty-five years now and of all of the weeks and months that make up those years I can only think about the past six months. Why me; why now; how could God... This food looks the same.

"Mr. Sinew, could you use some company?"

"Well Mrs. Wigren. It's always a pleasure to see your face and to hear your voice. Please, come on in."

"I can't stay very long, but I wanted to stop by your room on my way back front the dining room. Wasn't dinner delicious this evening? I have always liked the hash that we have here."

"Mrs. Wigren, do you ever have a bad word to say about anything?"

"Well, the ladies in the kitchen work so hard to prepare dinner for all of us I just feel that the right thing to do is to try to enjoy what they prepare. That's the way I was when I lived with my daughter. You've met my daughter haven't you Mr. Sinew? What I mean is that when you've lived alone for so many years as I had, you tend to get used to the way you cook so much that when someone else cooks for you it just doesn't satisfy your palate like your own cooking did."

"My wife, I've told you about my wife haven't I Mrs. Wigren? She used to cook a meal that would have lured Lazarus from his tomb, had she been cooking nearby."

"Oh Mr. Sinew, an old preacher like yourself, twisting the Bible so just to compliment your wife's cooking. You must have really loved her Mr. Sinew."

"That's true, Mrs. Wigren. I loved that woman with all my heart and would have gladly died in her place. She died last year you know; she had only been sick for a couple of months with congestion. Her heart just couldn't take it."

"I'm sorry Mr. Sinew. I surely didn't want to stir up such sad memories for you. I'd best be going back to my room now. I'll see you in the morning."

My wife was such a good woman. Why did she have to die? We were going to travel for a couple of years around the states. Why couldn't I have retired earlier? I should have given up that church long before. I wasn't any good for them; imagine, an old man like me trying to deliver a sermon of strength and comfort. I can't even get comfortable in this stupid bed. "Nurse! Nurse!"

"Yes Mr. Sinew. Are you o.k.?"

"There's nothing wrong with me. It's this awful bed. I can't relax with a bed that is raised up in the back like this!"

"Mr. Sinew, remember what we told you about the bed? If you want it to move so your head or your feet are in a different position all you have to do is use this hand control to adjust it. Remember that the blue button moves the head and the red button moves the foot of the bed. Here, like this."

"Are you sure that you told me about that? I don't remember anything at all about the bed moving."

"Yes sir, Mr. Sinew.

"Well, I don't remember anything about this stupid bed."

"Pardon Me. Mr. Sinew?"

"Ah, nothing. I'll try to keep it in mind this time." How was I supposed to know anything about this bed? At least, I don't believe that anyone has told me about the bed. My memory has been so bad that it is possible that they did. Sure they did you old fool! You're just too old to count on your own memory; you old fool.

"It's time for me to check your pulse and temperature Mr. Sinew. I also brought your medication for the evening."

"Come on in. I wouldn't mind the company for a few minutes."

"Have you been told that you'll be getting a new roommate tomorrow?"

"No, I don't believe so."

"Yes, Mr. Sears will be here from the hospital about 10:00 in the morning. He'll probably sleep most of the day from what I've heard about his condition so don't be alarmed if he doesn't speak to you until Wednesday. Well, your temperature and pulse are stable. All you need to do is take your medication and I'll get out of here so you can get to sleep."

"I suppose I should go to sleep. I'm feeling quite a bit more tired than usual."

"I'll see you tomorrow Mr. Sinew. Good night."

"Thank-you Nurse."

"Here's your breakfast Mr. Sinew. This orange juice should really perk you up."

"I hope so. It was difficult to wake up this morning. It must be because of this congestion around my heart. You know, young lady, age is the most determined of all the diseases. The doctors can prolong the inevitable; but in the long run, it'll get all of us. How old are you young lady?"

"I'm twenty-two Mr. Sinew."

"Twenty-two; I can remember when I was twenty-two. I was finishing up my seminary training just before I took my first church assignment. It was great to be young; but..."

"What's that Mr. Sinew?"

"I wish I had died then rather than to live such a hard life only to end up as the inevitable ending to some awful joke."

"Mr. Sinew, from what I've heard about you, you've lived a full life of travel, raising a family and helping other people. That doesn't sound like a joke. It sounds more like you were a very important part of this world and that without you it would have been a much harder place for a lot of people to have tried to live in."

"I did raise a son. His name was Eddie. He was always a good son who cared for people before. I had a chance to teach him that he should. He joined the Army when he was eighteen to try and help bring peace to this world; that was his reason, no matter how small a part he would play he wanted to play a part in it. He was killed when his plane was shot down in flight to Europe on his first mission to try and cause World War 2 to end more quickly."

"I'm sorry Mr. Sinew, I didn't know he had died. I'm sure that you were very proud of him."

"I loved him... I'm glad, in a way, that he did not have to face old age. I'd hate for anyone that I love to be this old."

"I have to get back to work Mr. Sinew. I'm sorry."

"Your new roommate just arrived Mr. Sinew, He's going to sleep for most of the day as we suspected."

"What seems to be wrong with him, other than being old like me?"

"He's only seventy Mr. Sinew, but he's had a rough time of it the past few months with a severe heart condition."

"He should pull through it then if he's only seventy. When I was seventy I was pastoring a large church in the center of town. I can remember when I was there; sometimes I felt there were not enough hours in the day. Now there seem to be way too many hours in the day. So many changes take place in one's life when old age moves in to stay."

"I think your roommate will be comfortable now. We'll be in to check on him often this morning to make sure that he's doing fine. I'll speak with you later Mr. Sinew."

He's only seventy. I bet he hates it that life seems to have cheated him out of the years he thought would be his to relax in. Those years for me were happy years until my Eve died. I'm glad I don't believe in reincarnation; I just couldn't go through losing her again. She was with me for most of my life. How could I possibly live without her?

"Mr. Sinew, would you like to go to church with us today down in the dining room? I thought today you might share with us some of your favorite scriptures from some of your sermons."

"No, I don't think so today. Besides, the only scriptures I can remember now-a days are those that are sad and depressing."

"Well, maybe if you come down with us, we can help you remember some of the more comforting and reassuring scriptures. From what I've heard about you, you were a strong leader of your church who believed in always helping others before doing something for yourself. I remember going to your church and listening to you preach about Heaven and how wonderful it would be to be in the presence of God."

"Old age has a way of causing one to forget the good things about the future and concentrating on the pain and sadness that surrounds him in the present. I can't sit and postulate about the possibilities of the future, I'm still trying to deal with the definite nature of my present."

"O.K. Mr. Sinew, Maybe tomorrow then. I'll stop back to see you then."

I can't be expected to carry the loads of others when my own burden is so heavy that I regret waking up in the morning to face it again. What has life become? It used to be, at least for me, a proving ground for accomplishment and a farmland for fulfilling experiences. Now it seems to have become, almost overnight, a juncture of fear, remorse, and almost constant loneliness. It doesn't matter if the room is full of visitors; it doesn't matter if I'm having a conversation with someone; loneliness at my heart with the fervor of a full construction crew. Like a lion facing death after reigning over his territory for more years than he can remember. I suppose circumstance must go on even if existence ceases.

"Your lunch is ready Mr. Sinew. Can I get you any juice to go with your lunch or would you just rather have milk again today?"

"I'll have the milk again today. The juice doesn't have a strong enough flavor to taste. At least I can still remember what milk is supposed to taste like so when I drink my imagination allows me to taste what I'm drinking."

"How about tomorrow I bring a wheel chair with me and I take you down to the dining room to eat with the group?"

"No!"

"I'm sorry Mr. Sinew. I did not want to upset you. I just thought you would like to talk with some of the other residents."

"I don't want to talk to the others. I'm depressed enough on my own without having to listen to the pains and problems of the rest of the world. Mrs. Wigren visits me in my room; she's the only conversationalist I care to deal with."

"That's alright Mr. Sinew, I'll leave your lunch and maybe you'll change your mind about it and want to go to the dining room on some other day."

"I doubt it, but thank-you." Will they ever learn that I don't want to listen to the world's problems anymore? Sixty-five long years as a minister was long enough. They were good years but I'm alone now and I just don't have the interest any longer. My Eve would understand. She would tell me to calm down, and to remember that the only reason I ever became a minister was to help people look past their own troubles to see there was always someone whose troubles were more catastrophic than their own, and that by helping someone else through their troubles it would make your own problems easier to deal with. She knew there were more reasons behind the decision I made so long ago, but that was one of the most important.

But now, it's different; I'm alone and my Eve is not here to be my friend. I just can't carry the weight of another human being; there have been so many.

"Mr. Sinew, I'm from the volunteer guild of the nursing home. I wanted to stop by to see if there might be someone you would like me to write a letter to for you? I know a lot of times it's difficult for some of the people living here to write and it's my small way of helping."

"That's very nice of you to offer, but the only person I write to anymore is my son, Eddie, and he will be visiting me just anytime now."

"That's great. Well, any time that you need for me to write for you just tell one of the nurses and they will get in touch with me, o.k.?"

"I sure will, and thank-you again for the offer." My Eddie will be by today I'm sure. When he does visit, I'll get him to move that clock a little closer so I can tell what time it is without asking around.

I think I can hear the dinner cart coming down the hallway. I sure am hungry; I'm not sure why they didn't bring me my lunch today. They must have been too busy to deal with all of the people so they let my lunch be one of those they just didn't serve.

"Here's your dinner Mr. Sinew. I hope you enjoy it."

"I'm hungry, I'm sure I will. You can't go without lunch and not be hungry at the end of the day."

"Mr. Sinew, you didn't go without lunch. Remember, I brought it to you myself today. I even offered to take you down to the dining room to eat with everyone else."

"I'm sure I had no lunch today. Maybe you're remembering yesterday?"

"No, Mr. Sinew; I was off work yesterday. It doesn't matter, if your real hungry and you eat all of your dinner, I'll bring you all of the extra portions you want."

"Thank-you." My memory is failing. So many changes from the way things used to be. It's so hard to keep up.

"Hello Mr. Sinew. It's time for me to check your vital signs and to give you your medicine. How are you this evening?"

"I'm fine, I suppose. Have you seen Mrs. Wigren today? She has been in the habit of visiting me each day and I've not seen her today. Is she visiting her family at their home?"

"Mrs. Wigren wasn't feeling very well this morning so she has stayed in bed all day."

"Will she be alright?"

"Her doctor is scheduled to visit her tomorrow morning but I think he has already made up his mind since she has been so lucky in the past, that this time she may not have the strength to come back."

Oh my God! She's going to die too! I thought that she would be exempt from death since she was such a sweet lady and so helpful to everyone she met, "Her family must be heart - broken."

"She has no living relatives that we know about; but, anyone that has known her like we have I'm sure will feel a great loss."

Will death never be satisfied? Will the grave never be vanquished? So many good people die before they have done the things they still have planned to do. My Eve was so full of life until the last moment. She would have completed those courses at the University had she not taken ill so quickly. What's next? Is this the way I'm to view what life I have left? It's just not fair.

"Mr. Sinew, I'm Mrs. Sears. My husband is your new roommate."

"Good morning Mrs. Sears. How is your husband?"

"He's still sleeping. They told me when I arrived this morning that he has slept the entire time he has been here from the hospital."

"As far as I know he has."

"I was told that you are a minister."

"I used to be. Now I'm just a patient like your husband."

"Oh, my husband sold real-estate. He retired at sixty-five and he and I have been traveling around the country ever since. I was really surprised when the doctors said his heart was failing him and the only chance he had to live was to undergo corrective surgery. My man could not have lived if he could not continue to do all of the things he was so used to doing. So, he chose to have the surgery. I'm so frightened that he'll not survive. He's my life and has been for fifty years."

"Mrs. Sears, you and your husband sound like you were always very much in love. That is a treasure that even death cannot steal. God gave love to man because it was the one prize that God Himself cherished more than any other. He loves us and he gave us this treasure that we might enjoy the feeling that He enjoys in loving us by our being able to love someone else."

"Oh Mr. Sinew, you are still a wonderful minister."

"Well, when my memory doesn't fade."

"Thank-you. I think I'll go and be with my husband now."

It's so easy to share words of strength with someone else and yet so hard to listen to their meaning for myself.

"Mr. Sinew, here's your breakfast."

"Thank-you. It sure smells good this morning."

"I hope it tastes as good as it smells."

"Please, someone, get a Nurse... My husband, please get a Nurse!"

"I'll call for one Mrs. Sears! I need a nurse stat! They'll hear the call from their station board and be here as quickly as possible."

"Who's in need?"

"It's my husband Nurse! He's not breathing! Help HIM!!"

"Mrs. Sears, it appears that your husband has been gone for about a half an hour... I'm very sorry. I'll cover his face and then go and call his doctor."

"No! Don't cover his face! I want to be with him for a few more minutes before... my sweet man."

"I suppose it's over for us. I have loved you more than anything or anyone in my entire life. Please wait for me somewhere in the stars; I can't live for very long without you with me. Remember our first date my love? You took me to see Gone with the Wind, and now you're gone."

"Mrs. Sears, why don't you come with me while the doctor takes care of your husband?"

"You know that's true dear, you'll always be my husband. I love you; good-bye."

"Nurse."

"Yes Mr. Sinew?"

"Would you please take my breakfast tray, I'm not very hungry now."

"Sure. Mr. Sinew; will you be alright?"

"I will be in a few minutes. Please don't worry about me, just take care of Mrs. Sears. Right now she is the loneliest person in the world."

They've taken Mr. Sears away. I feel so sorry for his wife and what she is going through right now. The sting of death is still felt by those who loved and are left behind only with their memories. I'm glad that my memory has failed me at times. Sometimes memories can make it all too real that the one we had loved for so many years is gone from our lives forever. I hope Mrs. Sears and her husband can meet somewhere in the stars as she hopes.

"Hello Mr. Sinew. Will you be going down to church with us today?"

"I don't believe so. My Eddie is to visit me this morning and I don't want to miss him. Thank-you though."

"Are you sure Mr. Sinew? I didn't think that Eddie was able to visit you."

"Oh yes, he'll be here. He's always been reliable; in fact, my Eve used to say that you could set a clock by that boy."

"Maybe tomorrow then Mr. Sinew."

"Could you please tell the kitchen that I'm not very hungry for lunch today, so for them to not send me a tray today."

"I sure will. I'll see you later."

When Eddie gets here, I need to ask him if he'll bring that clock a little closer to the bed so I can tell the time more easily.

"Nurse, could you please come down to my room when you get the chance. There's no emergency, I just have a question for you."

"I'll be right down Mr. Sinew."

"How can I help you Mr. Sinew?"

"I have not seen Mrs. Wigren for two days now. Has she gone home to live with her family?"

"No Mr. Sinew, she has not gone home to live with her family. She passed away last night in her sleep. I wanted to wait a couple of days before telling you since your roommate left us just today. I'm sorry; she was a great lady and so very nice."

"I'm sure that after a long visit with her family that she'll be back to visit me."

"Mr. Sinew... can I get you anything?"

"No thank-you, I'm expecting company in a few minutes; if I need anything I just ask them if they would get it for me."

"O.K., you call me if you need me."

It's been such a long day. I'm really looking forward to my nap this afternoon. Eddie will be here for a while around lunchtime. I'll wait 'til he leaves before I take my nap.

"I'm going to change the bedding today Mr. Sinew. I'll change the other bed first and when I've finished it, I'll help you move over to the chair and I'll change yours."

"That's fine with me. Clean bed sheets always feel so fresh." I can remember when my Eve would change the bedding on a bright spring day. The fresh smell of outside air where they had hung to dry would fill the bedroom with such a good feeling. I'm glad that Eve is going to stop by today to visit; I miss her so much. It seems like such a long time since I held her in my aims and told her I love her. I must do that today when she visits."

"I've finished with this one Mr. Sinew. Are you ready to move over to the chair?"

"That'll be fine. I can look out the window better from the chair."

"Let's use the walker just in case. There, that wasn't too hard."

"Yes, this is fine."

There are birds in that tree. Several of them on that one branch. They sing such a pretty song this time of day. I think they are sparrows; it's hard to tell without my glasses though. Oh, they're all flying away except for one lone bird. I wonder why he did not fly away with the others? What? it's fallen to the ground. It must have died. That one bird, left all alone on the branch because it was dead. I suppose nothing escapes death. Some things or people are suffered to die a more physically painful death than others while some are decreed to dye much lonelier deaths. Is there anything more painful than loneliness? Is there anything more devastating than growing old only to see all of those you have grown to know and love dye before you, leaving you to remember daily the pain of losing them?

I can't feel anything now. What has happened? A moment ago I could at least feel pain, sorrow and loss. Now I have no sensation at all. Is this to last for long or am I dying at this very moment? That must be it; I'm dying. Oh, so lonely... "My God, My God, have you forsaken me?"

"Mr. Sinew? Mr. Sinew?"

ULTIMA CHANZA

"Help me'" begged a voice from the rear of the wreckage. "Dear God, am I pinned here to die?"

What should I do now? I came to these God-forsaken mountains to free myself from other people. Now, it looked like I was being forced to share my hermitage with an unknown. I could just leave him there. He would die in a day or two anyway.

"Help me'" cried the voice.

"Bull!" I sighed.

"Is there someone there?" questioned the voice. "God has provided for my need. Thank-you, dear God'"

I tossed pieces of the fuselage aside as I made my way back to my unwanted guest. A brown-haired, bearded man was entangled by the sides of the formless plane. Still silent, I started ripping away at the torn metal. I finally freed this thorn that was already pressuring my back-side.

His religious babbling was unending. "You are God-called just to save me; so very thankful to you and my God for saving my life; I almost died."

His foolishness grew to point where I could no longer stand it. When we reached the outside of the plane, I firmly told him, "Shut your bloody mouth'"

The expression on his face brought back memories. One specific time in a small section of Tombstone, Arizona, called Entrada al Inferno. I had just rolled a suit-and-tie business man and then shot off his right ear because he only had thirty dollars. What a time I had then.

I felt extremely happy about the solitude that I had found in the Ultima Chanza Mountains. There was no temptation to talk to anyone before. Now though, things were changing. The mere presence of this religious fanatic stirred a desire inside of me to talk; at this point, to anyone. Literally. By nightfall, I began to cook some of the food I had found on the plane. I carried both plates over to where he was sitting. He just sat there-his head hurried between his knees.

"Eat this before you starve to death," I told him.

"What do you care if I die or not?" he mumbled.

"Just eat it," I said.

I watched as he slowly raised his head and eventually took the plate.

"Who are you anyways?" I asked after waiting some twenty minutes.

"I am of God," he answered proudly.

An anger began to grow inside. I tried once more to make simple conversation. "Where are you from?"

He replied, "If I say that I am of God, then I must be from Heaven.

"Come on," I yelled, "don't start that again. You know as well as I do there is no Heaven."

"But that's not true," he argued. "God created a Heaven just as he created the Earth."

"You're ridiculous," I told him, "There's no way that I'm gonna stay here and listen to this gibberish you call religion. Just no way." With that, I walked toward the woods.

"Stop, my brother; listen to me," were the last words I heard from the Christian.

I was sure now that I should have let him die in that plane. Jesus, did I ever complicate my life this time. It wasn't bad enough that I had to leave Tombstone for killing some Holy-Roller preacher. Now my hiding place had been invaded by some clown on a religious kick.

All I could think about was how stupid I was by letting him live. What was wrong with me? I could take care of that problem very easily. I could just go back to camp and kill him, I destroyed a human pest before; I could do it again.

I decided to circle around behind the camp to catch him by surprise. I took out my belt to use as a weapon and began my mission.

The woods had become thick with weeds and bushes. I was just guessing where to walk as the darkness began to surround me. As I was nearing me destination, my right foot slipped and I began to fall. I fell fast and then was stopped suddenly. My belt had caught hold of something atop the cliff I had fallen over. All I could see was the river hundreds of feet below me with the moon shining over it.

Now I knew why the Spanish Name Ultima Chanza had been given to these mountains. The world had been given one last chance to successfully kill me. It wasn't enough that I was beaten-up a hundred times in Entrada al Inferno. It wasn't enough that I was badgered by pushers and pimps to join up with them. Now I was to die a tragic death by falling into the bolder infested river.

I can't believe it. How could that Christian profess to believe in a protector? Someone or thing who's supposed to keep people from danger. I guess a few sick weaklings who call themselves men need something to believe in. If I believed in anything except for myself, I would have been cheated and lied to much more than I ever was.

If there was a God, why would he let something that he created be tortured by earthly forces? If there was a God, why would he stand by and let his creation be killed? If there was a God, then he's really ripped me off this time. Then I blacked-out.

When I awoke, I was lying atop the cliff, I stood and looked around. There was no one to be seen.

What had happened? I couldn't remember any anything after I blacked-out. "My belt; where's my..." it was still hanging on the cliff's edge. I reached for it and barely touched it when the small twig it had hung onto snapped and the belt fell towards the river. How could that twig have held me? How did I get up here? Why was I still alive? There's no way I could have climbed up here even if the belt had held me. The Christian; he saved my life. I turned toward the camp site to see that the fire had burned out. I began to run toward the area of the camp. As I came closer to the camp, I saw the Christian sitting exactly in the spot I had left him. I stopped, and looked at him wondering why he had let the fire burn out. Still hidden from his sight, I threw a stone to the far side of the camp. When it struck a tree, the Christian was startled.

"Is that you?" said the Christian, He still did not move, I threw another stone to a different palace.

"Hey, don't tease me!" he pleaded. Slowly he began to move. He was crawling with a great amount of pain. Just as I thought, his leg had been broken from the plane crash. There was no way possible that he could have pulled me to the top even if he could have gotten there in time.

"Are you out there?" Lord Jesus, guard me in my time of need," pray of the Christian.

I walked into the camp and headed for my tent.

"It was you," said the Christian.

I stopped in front of my tent and said, "Were you the only one on the plane?" I asked him.

"Of course not," he replied.

"You weren't," I exclaimed. "Who was with you? Where is he now?"

The Christian replied," My co-pilot was God and he's with us right now."

"You're ridiculous!" I screamed, "Completely ridiculous," I rushed into my tent in search of seclusion from my Christian neighbor-the psychopathic fool.

I laid flat on my cot, trying to sleep. But my eyes wouldn't stay shut for more than a minute. I thought at first that my reason for not being able to sleep was the Christian. That was only part of it. I was so puzzled about why I was still alive. I had been close to death many times before; but, never had the odds been so against me. Maybe when I blacked-out, I accomplished some super-human feat of strength. I've heard about such things when people do the impossible where their life depend on it. Sure, that's what it was. For a moment there I became superman and that's all there is to it.

All night long I tossed and turned. It was almost sunrise when I fell from my cot with a scream. Cold sweat was running down my face and neck. My eyes were frozen in a shock-like stare. I had relived my fall at the cliff. Only this time, I fell completely experiencing the fall through the air. It was strange though, on impact it felt as though a feather cushion had been placed there to protest me from injury.

When I came to my senses again, I heard the Christian yelling, "Are you alright, my brother?"

"Sure" I said. "I'm alright."

The experiences of the last two days were too much for me. I was trembling with nervousness constantly. As I drank my coffee, the Christian began to drag himself out to the fire from the plane wreckage where he slept.

"Good morning, my brother," he said. His voice showed signs of pain from his broken leg; but still, there was an over shadow of peace and harmony. "You're not talking this morning are you? Well, I talk to you then. The supplies should last us a week or so. That will be plenty of time for us to make it to the nearest town to find a doctor."

"You came here alone. If you want to leave, leave by yourself," I said.

"But my leg is broken," he argued with his still harmonious voice. "I can hardly move ten feet and you expect me to travel fifty miles to Tombstone."

"Where?" I growled. "I thought that you said that you had no memory of anything."

"I said anything except God," he answered.

"So, what does your God have to do with anything?" I said.

"I prayed to him and said if it was his will for me to return home, for Him to tell me where it was," he explained.

"Well," I said, "he really stuck it to you this time, buddy."

"What do you mean by that?" he asked.

"There's no way you can go back to Tombstone," I said.

"Why not?" he asked.

"Because I killed a man there and there were three witnesses who saw the whole thing," I replied.

"It's God's will that I go to Tombstone. So, He'll work it out," said the Christian.

"Why don't you shut-up about God for today," I pleaded. "I've got enough on my mind the way it is already."

"If you wish," replied the Christian.

What's going on? He wouldn't shut-up before. Why Now? Maybe he's demon possessed. I laughed out loud.

"What's so funny?" said the Christian.

"Oh, nothing really," I answered. "I just had a funny thought."

"Would you like to share it?" said the Christian.

"I don't think so," I replied.

"Would you like to talk about whatever is bothering you?" asked the Christian.

"What makes you think that something is wrong with me?" I asked.

"You're shaking like a leaf," he said, "If you shake much more, you'll scald yourself even worse than you already have with that coffee."

I couldn't believe it. He actually seemed concerned about me. "What's it to you if I did scald myself?" I said.

"I'm interested in you," he said. "I want to know your thoughts and feelings about things."

"Why?" I asked him.

"I feel that it's my job to get to know you and understand you," he answered.

"Your job? What do you mean by that?"

"I'm not sure," he said. "I've had this thought all day long."

"What's that?" I asked.

"That God has a purpose for me being here. I don't really know what it is; but he'll show me soon."

That thought was too much for me. I just sat quietly, thinking for a while. This man was in severe pain; and yet, he was so peaceful looking. His voice had even lost its underlying tone of pain. What is it that compelled him to be so concerned for me?

For the rest of the night, only a few words past between us. No conversation was started at all. When the moon was high, I went to my tent for the evening. Again I tossed endlessly in my cot. I was again falling from that cliff. This time the wind was causing great pain to my face and arms. But it wasn't a wind burn; it was extreme heat; like fire blazing all around me. The further I fell, the hotter it became. Just as I was about to hit the rock covered river, I rolled from my cot to the floor. The shock of the fall made me scream with terror. Then silence again took over, The Christian didn't ask about me this time. But I heard some noise coming from the plane.

As I neared the plane, it was the Christian praying out loud. "Dear God, my God," he said, "I pray to you in Jesus' name, to take this pain from my leg forever. I pray to you, my Lord, with the faith that you have control over all that is-even my unbelieving brother who saved me."

Before he could state his next sentence, I heard his voice speaking in a strange foreign language. He spoke at first and then began to shout and almost sing in the same unknown language. I then heard noises from the plane. The noises sounded like metal in the plane was being moved around and beat upon. "He must have gone crazy," I said in a whisper. After standing there for too long I felt, I ran back to my tent. I could still hear the muffled noises from the plane for almost an hour. Then, silence took over.

The morning of the third day was fair and sunny. I walked from my tent toward the camp fire. It was already burning and a pot of coffee sitting on it. A noise from behind me made me turn with a start. It was the Christian walking out of the woods.

"Fresh rabbit for breakfast," he said.

"You're walking," I screamed. "You had a broken leg just yesterday. I saw it myself."

"I had a broken leg," he said. "But now it is healed. Completely healed by the almighty God."

"How can that be?" I cried. "I...you..." I began to cry. I had no idea what to do next, I had seen for myself his badly infected and broken leg. But now it was totally healed with no sign of injury. There had to be a God. There was just no way on Earth for a leg to get well by itself like that.

"Help me to understand," I begged. "I'm in need of something and don't even know what."

"You're in need of God my brother," said the Christian. "Believe in Him. That's all it takes. His love for you is there, you just need to accept it."

"How do I know He loves me?" I cried. "What has He ever done for me?"

"He saved your life," replied the Christian," and gave you a last chance to accept the free gift of salvation."

"What good will God's love do me now," I asked. "I'm a wanted man. I'm a murderer. When I go back, I'll be hung'"

The Christian's eyes closed and then his body collapsed to the ground. That same wild language came from his lips. Only this time, it seemed as if he were talking directly to me. His body began to tremble and contract as the wild tongues grew louder.

His body stopped its uncontrollable quivering at the same moment as the unknown language stopped, I stared at the Christians body lying limp on the ground. With one great jerk, the body sprang to its feet. A deep, rich voice burst from the Christian's mouth. A voice totally different from the Christian's voice. It said, "I am the light and the truth. I am the alpha and the omega. I am called Jesus. Repent: for the Kingdom of Heaven is at hand. It is written, thou shalt worship the Lord thy God, and Him shalt thou serve. Blessed are the pure in heart: for they shall see God."

I fell to my knees and cried, "Don't destroy me. I beg of you, don't kill me.

"Why are ye fearful?" the voice said. "Ye of little faith. Ye have heard that it was said by them of old time, thou shalt not kill; and whosoever shall kill shall be in danger of the judgement. That is true, but ye have killed no one. The man ye fear to be dead is now standing before you and it is through his mouth that I now speak. Go back to your home and begin anew.

"Lay not up for yourself treasures upon earth, where moth and rust doth corrupt, and where thieves break through and steal: but lay up for yourself treasures in Heaven, where neither moth nor rust doth corrupt, and where thieves do not break through nor steal. For where your treasures are, there will your heart be also.

"Let your light so shine before men, that they may see your good works, and glorify your father which is in Heaven.

"Follow Me my son. Follow Me."

I cried, "I will try with all of my heart, my Lord."

Then the voice said, "Peace be unto you."

A NEW NAME – STAGE PLAY

Saul Thompson: man on the bench

Carol Thompson: his wife

John Thompson: their son

Barbie Thompson: their daughter

Judd   best friend

Hobo

Unknown girl

As the curtain opens, a well-dressed, well-groomed, middle-aged man sits alone on an old but sturdy park bench that sits at the front of the stage, left. This area of the stage is dimly lit by the solitary streetlight positioned at the back of the stage, center. Another park bench sits directly below the light. Front stage, right, sits part of an old moss covered bridge that stretches completely off stage, right. A scarce amount of light shines over the bridge from the centered light in the back of the park.

A well-dressed, middle-aged woman walks onto the stage from the left and stands near the park bench.

> Carol Thompson
>
> I've been looking all over for you. What are you doing here?

> Saul Thompson
>
> Waiting to die.

Carol Thompson

Waiting for what?

Saul Thompson

To die. In a few minutes I'm going over to that bridge and jump into the river.

Carol Thompson

But darling, you have so much to lose by killing yourself.

Saul Thompson

I can't seem to think of one thing.

Carol Thompson

What about me? What about the love we've shared for twenty-three years?

Saul Thompson

We did share a love; but that was fifteen years ago, Fifteen years ago-that's when I began to die. I've really been dead for seven years now, but there wasn't anyone around with the decency to even bury me.

Carol Thompson

Fifteen years ago?' That's when life really began. That was the year you were promoted to the second vice president's position in the company. Then we were able to move into the best part of town; associate with the best people. We became the best; the best.

Saul Thompson

That's where we much different from each other, Carol. I would work hard for the things we had and was very proud of them, because I had never had anything like them before. But you? You were proud of them because you had them and no one else did. You weren't even satisfied with the idea of being as well-off as our neighbors. You had to have more than they did.

Carol Thompson
What do I have to do to make you know that I still love you the way I did when we were first married?

Saul Thompson
Tell me that you'll sell all of your jewelry and furs. That we can give away all of the money we have, and start anew--as poor people.

Carol Thompson
But Saul, you've worked so hard for the things that we have. And not just that, but (shakes her head) I couldn't survive without the luxuries that I've grown to love.

Saul Thompson
All the more reason for me to take my life. I've programed and destroyed your life, and you don't even realize it. It's true; if you were taken away from the tragically luxurious life you're living now, you probably would die. Oh, but what a pure death it would be.

Carol Thompson
Saul, maybe you should see a doctor. A specialist in fact. He could help you to forget these crazy things you are saying.

Saul Thompson
I already have an appointment with the only doctor who can help me now. His office is just below that bridge. He specializes in death.

Carol Thompson
(Turns her back to him and begins to walk stage right)

"I've got to run. Don't stay around here too long, we're expected at Jefferson's at seven."

Saul Thompson
You never did take what I said seriously. Of course I didn't expect you to. Your life is too regulated by dollar signs and checking account numbers to understand a real thought when one comes at you.

Carol Thompson
Remember Saul, seven o'clock.

(She exits stage right)

Saul Thompson
(Talking to himself)

My poor Carol. Too money hungry to even think of death; or for that matter, anything in the real world.

(He sits on the bench silently for a few minutes, then a young man walks on stage from the bench.)

John Thompson
Good evening father.

(He squeaks coldly)

Saul Thompson
John?

John Thompson
When you didn't make it to the Jefferson's, mother got in touch with me and told me where you were.

Saul Thompson

And why did she send you down here? I told her that my mind was made. I'm going to end it all tonight.

John Thompson

Well, mother now believes that you are going to kill yourself. She also feels that you are mad at her for some reason, and wants to make sure that, ah; well, that you haven't made out a will that would leave her with nothing.

Saul Thompson

Oh my God. I thought that you and I would never talk about money in this way. What happened between us? We, of all people, had a good thing. We used to go fishing and camping almost every weekend. We played baseball and tennis together. We used to go swimming at the beach before breakfast all thru the year. I even made sure that you were able to attend graduate school at Yale seven years ago. Now that I think about it, that's when our relationship ceased to exist. I should have known. You were too much like your mother to be able to remain the same in the atmosphere that exists at Yale, but why? Why did you change so drastically?

John Thompson

You always taught me that for a business man to get anywhere in the world, he had to change with the times. That's all I did, I changed with the times.

Saul Thompson

But I'm not talking about the business world son. I'm talking about the world of life. The world of leisure and enjoyment, not the world of facts and figures.

John Thompson

Is there a way to successfully have one without the other?

Saul Thompson

(Sadly)

I suppose not. That's why I'm doing what I am. A world without leisure and enjoyment is a dead world, and since I'm living in a dead world, I might as well be dead.

John Thompson

If that's what you want, Mr. Thompson.

Saul Thompson

(Surprised)

Mr. Thompson?

John Thompson

Yes. Mr. Thompson, we have business to attend to.

Saul Thompson

Tell your mother, Mrs. Thompson, that she doesn't have to worry about ever going without money. It's all hers. She can have it all.

John Thompson

(Reaching out his hand)

The business world is losing a giant.

Saul Thompson

(Turning his head away from his son and not attempting to shake his hand)

Don't worry. There's an idiot born every minute. Now leave me alone.

(John exits stage right. A young girl in a tennis outfit, all out eighteen, walks on stage from the left. She is accompanied by a young man of about the same age,)

Barbie Thompson

Hi Daddy. Mother said that this is where you'd be.

Saul Thompson

My little Barbie, You're so sweet. When did you talk to your mother?

Barbie Thompson

She was looking for John at the country club, and they paged me instead.

Saul Thompson

Oh; who's your friend dear?

Barbie Thompson

This is Hunt. You know his dad, Huntington McAlister, of the First National Bank of Beverly Hills.

Saul Thompson

(He sighs)

Yes, I know him.

Barbie Thompson

Wait for me by the car.

(The young man steps off stage, right.)

Daddy dear, mother told me what you had on your mind.

Saul Thompson

Yes?

Barbie Thompson

Well, you remember when you told me that you would buy me that Jaguar Elite? I just wanted to make sure I could still get it.

Saul Thompson

The other two I can believe it out of, but not you. You were different from those two from the start.

Barbie Thompson

It's not that Daddy. I figured that if I had a Jaguar Elite, Hunt's parents would see that I wasn't after their son for his money. Mother doesn't want me to marry him at all, so she won't do it for me.

Saul Thompson

Whatever cover you put on it, it still reads the same. You have the same love for money that your mother has.

(He sits silent for a moment, then says)

Leave me alone.

Barbie Thompson

But what about the car?

(She growls harshly).

Saul Thompson

(Almost threatening he says)

Leave me alone.

(Barbie runs off stage right, crying. Her boyfriend is heard saying)

Did you get the car?

                    Barbie Thompson

(Growling)

Oh, shut up and drive.

(Saul Thompson is left sitting alone on the park bench)

(From stage left, a man of the same age as Saul Thompson runs toward the bench)

                          Judd

Thank God, I'm not too late.

                    Saul Thompson

Judd, what are you doing here?

                          Judd

Carol told me that you were planning to do away with yourself. I had to hurry to get here before you went through with it.

                    Saul Thompson

My mind is made up. You can't talk me out of it.

                          Judd

That's not what I'm here for. What a man does with his own life is his own business.

                    Saul Thompson

Then what are you doing here?

                          Judd

I know it's not exactly the right time to say this; but, if you die everything will go to Carol. And the first thing she'll do is sell your cottage on the lake. That would almost be like murder to sell that place. I have too many memories of the times I spent there, to see it sold right out from under my feet, knowing that there's not a thing that I can do about it.

Saul Thompson
(Almost as if he is sick to his stomach)

Man, you are sick.

Judd
All you have to do is to sign this release and the place is mine, all mine. Just this one last favor for an old friend. How about it?'

Saul Thompson
Anything to get you out of here.

(He signs the paper.)

Judd
Thanks, old man,

(He runs off stage right)

I can make it to my lawyer's office before...

(Saul shakes his head with disgust)

(A man comes on stage from the left.)

Hobo
(He talks calm and confidently)

You mind if I sit here? Hey, you alright?

Saul Thompson
(Very dazed)

Huh, oh-ah, yeah, go ahead and sit down.

Hobo

Thanks. You come here much?

Saul Thompson

No; and this probably my last visit

Hobo

That's a shame. The park is a beautiful place to be if you can't be in the real wilderness. A small part of the real world transplanted into this concrete prison.

Saul Thompson

(Saul isn't really listening to a word that the Hobo is saying)

Hobo

Since my escape from this prison, life has been good to me. No tension or stress caused by synthetic worry. In fact, I could safely say that my heart beat has slowed down to amost half the speed of what it used to be.

Saul Thompson

You don't say.

Hobo

It's true, And to top it off, I'm not only healthier, but much more educated in what makes the world go around. The freedom that is enjoyed by all of the animals of the earth is over-whelming, They live happy, healthy, and productive lives by being a part of nature, My whole purpose in life is to pattern myself after them. After all, I'm one of the earth's creatures too.

Saul Thompson

That's true,

Hobo

Well, I'll be leaving you now. I think I'll go back there to that bench and take a little nap. Tomorrow is another day and I need to rest up for it. It's been nice talking to you.

Saul Thompson

Yeah, sure.

(The Hobo gets up and walks to the back of the stage where he lies down on the bench and remains there quietly.)

(Saul gets up and slowly walks towards the bridge. As he gets to the center of the stage, a young girl in her early twenties runs onto the stage from off stage right. She stands on the bridge and cries. At the next moment she begins to climb onto the side of the bridge.)

Saul Thompson

Hey Wait!

(Saul runs to the bridge and takes hold of the girl just as she begins to leap toward the river.)

Unknown girl

(Crying)

Let me go, there's nothing left—I've got to go through with it.

Saul Thompson

Just Wait, Let's talk for a minute.

Unknown girl

(She cries in a frantic voice)

There's nothing to talk about. Let me go.

                    Saul Thompson
Maybe I need someone to talk to myself. Give me a
chance – just a chance.

(The girl stops jerking about and stands still beside Saul)

There now, that's better. What's your name?

                    Unknown girl
(Sharply, still crying)

It doesn't matter.

                    Saul Thompson
Okay, it doesn't matter then.

(He pauses for a moment)

Let's be honest. You've got a large problem that you're
sure that only death can solve, right?

                    Unknown girl
Right.

(Still crying)

But you can't help me, No one can.

                    Saul Thompson
Give me a chance. Some people feel I have accomplished
a lot in in my time.

                    Unknown girl
It's my son. He was in a car accident and will die unless
he is operated on within the next month, I was driving,
I was...

(Crying)

Saul Thompson

You can't afford the operation? Is that it?

Unknown girl

That's it. Now let me go!

Saul Thompson

Hold on now. How much will the operation cost?

Unknown girl

At least $50,000. There are only three specialists who can perform the operation and all three are in Europe.

(A pause of silence)

Saul Thompson

Here, take this.

Unknown girl

(Amazed)

It's a blank check.

(Paused again)

How I pray that you have enough money to back it up.

Saul Thompson

Believe me, I do have enough to back it up. Take it and use it well. But...

Unknown girl

(With a sad laugh)

I knew that there had to be a catch. But I don't care; whatever you want me to do--anything, My son's only ten years old, the idea of life is still new to him.

Saul Thompson

That's the qualification. Make sure that the idea of life is always new to him. Don't let him end up on a bridge in some park as we have. Encourage him to live as all of Earth's creatures should; enjoy the happy, healthy, and productive life of being a part of the natural world.

Unknown girl

(Surprised)

Is that all?

Saul Thompson

Don't take it lightly. It's hard to do. It's hard to be sure of one's natural freedom.

(With a fresh smile on her face, the girl runs off stage, left. When she is completely off of the stage, Saul walks slowly off to the left. He then looks toward the back of the stage. Then slowly takes off his suit coat, and tie; throws them towards the bridge, and walks toward the now sleeping Hobo. When he reaches bench, the Hobo awakens.)

Saul Thompson

You mind if I sit here?

Hobo

Sure Paul.

Saul Thompson

That's good. A new life ... a new name.

DISPATCHER – SCREEN PLAY

FADE IN:

EXT. DARK, DESERTED AND NARROW ALLEY WITH ONLY A HINT OF DIFUSED LIGHT COMING FROM THE OPEN END OF THE ALLEY - A LONE STREET LAMP ACROSS THE STREET. WITH THE APPEARANCE OF MIDNIGHT, THE DISTANT SOUNDS OF A CITY CAN BE HEARD IN THE BACKGROUND.

An adult female, brunette, who looks to be about 30 years old, and clearly attractive beneath the fresh blood and numerous bruises, is alone and lying between several garbage cans, some overturned and all looking battered and well used. She hardly moves as she begins slowly talking to herself.

> DISPATCHER
> It won't be long now I'm sure.

She's very short of breath as she speaks.

> DISPATCHER
> I've seen death - plenty of it. But I never realized dying could be so painful.

Her face contorts first from pain and then resolves into an expression of acceptance.

> DISPATCHER
> But I'd rather die; rather die than; than to keep playing his horrible game.

> CUT TO:

INT. ELEGENT BUSINESS OFFICE. ALL FOUR WALLS ARE COMPLETELY GLASS, FLOOR TO CEILING, WITH NO WALL HANGINGS. ALL THAT CAN BE SEEN THROUGH THE GLASS IS SLOW MOVING SMOKE THAT COMPLETELY SURROUNDS THE OFFICE. THERE IS A LARGE, EXECUTIVE DESK WITH WEATHERED, REDLEATHER INLAYS POSITIONED IN ONE CORNER OF THE OFFICE. A HIGH-BACKED, RED LEATHER CHAIR SITS BEHIND THE DESK WITH ITS BACK TO THE CORNER AND A SINGLE LOW-BACKED, RED LEATHER CHAIR IN FRONT OF THE DESK. THERE ARE NO VISIBLE LIGHTS IN THE OFFICE, BUT IT IS WELL LIGHTED.

Dispatcher sits alone in the low-backed, red leather chair on the visitor's side of the desk. Numerous screams and cries of pain and agony can be faintly heard in the background - muffled by the office walls.

> DISPATCHER (Voice Over - VO)
> It's hard to believe that at one time, a very long time ago, I was quite content to represent this place.

She turns her head slowly and looks at the surrounding windows.

> DISPATCHER (VO)
> Now though, it's really difficult to deal with the screams and moans that surround this office.

She pauses and listens for a moment.

> DISPATCHER (VO)
>
> It's more difficult knowing; knowing that I helped to put some of them in here.

She stands and walks close to the windows, walking slowly around the office, looking painfully out into the smoke.

> DISPATCHER (VO)
>
> Most of these people wouldn't be here if my boss had stayed out of their lives.

She reaches out her hand and touches a window.

> DISPATCHER (VO)
>
> This is where I come in. My job. And my job's always been clear. She slowly leans into the window letting her head gently rest against the glass.

> DISPATCHER (VO)
>
> My boss sends me out to screw up people's lives.

She pauses.

> DISPATCHER (VO)
>
> I'm supposed to fix it so they lose all hope. Lose all hope that they can ever overcome their problems and have a better life.

With her head still against the glass, her eyes slowly pan back and forth. She speaks with a tone of sadness and remorse.

DISPATCHER (VO)

They're usually damned by their reactions - before they even know what hit'em.

She moves back to the chair and sits with a sad, exhausted breath. She speaks with a tone of concern.

DISPATCHER (VO)

I'm not sure how long I can continue to modify my orders.

A wry smile crosses her face.

DISPATCHER (VO)

It's easy enough to outsmart the idiot minions who follow me. They're always trying to catch me red-handed; huh, so to speak.

The smile leaves her face is replaced by a look of overwhelming fear.

DISPATCHER (VO)

But even though the Boss is not omniscient, he's not stupid either.

She slowly shakes her head.

DISPATCHER (VO)

But his orders are so malignant; so vicious, so - I just can't follow those orders. I can't...

She turns her head and looks out the portion of the window she was just standing near. Her tone has returned to sadness and remorse.

                    DISPATCHER (VO)
    If I went through with them as ordered, lives would
    continue to be destroyed just because...

She pauses as she turns her head away from the window.

                    DISPATCHER (VO)
    I sheepishly followed orders.

The door to the office opens and as it does, the screams
and moans become instantly louder.

A well-dressed, confident looking man enters the office,
closing the door behind him. He looks to be about 35, six
feet- three, broad-shouldered with a very agile, athletic
look about him. He walks calmly to the high-backed, red
leather chair behind the desk and sits. He speaks with a
smooth tone and an almost sweet pronunciation of each
syllable. His speech and expression are often laced with
a myriad of emotions.

He opens his talk with Dispatcher with clearly spoken
insincerity.

                    THE BOSS
    Well Dispatcher. It's always good to see you looking
    so - tempting.

He pauses and looks at the woman with an expression
of controlled, ravenous hunger.

                    THE BOSS
    I've just completed your next list of orders.

He pauses again. His look changes to one of bored
disinterest.

> THE BOSS
>
> In the past, you've had some shaky excuses about why your assignments were not being completed as planned - by this office.

He stands and turns his back to her. Now with a satisfied look etched on his face, he gazes out one of the back windows.

> THE BOSS
>
> Yes. I like what I see.

Still facing the window, his expression changes to a look of disgust.

> THE BOSS
>
> Listen carefully Dee. This is your last chance. If you fail to complete these orders, you'll be transferred back to this location. All privileges stripped.

He turns from the window, still wearing a look of disgust. He appears to be attempting to burn a look right through Dee.

> THE BOSS
>
> This would be a permanent transfer. One with no appeal.

He pauses. His expression now moves from disgust to barely bridled anger.

> THE BOSS
>
> Do I make myself understood?

He pauses. His expression of anger slithers into a fake, overly accommodating smile.

THE BOSS

Of course you understand?

He pauses. His look returns to an expression of controlled, ravenous hunger.

THE BOSS

Of course you do.

He slowly walks around the desk and stands very near Dee, nearly breathing the same air she is breathing.

THE BOSS

One of the reasons you were picked for this duty was your extreme intelligence.

His eyes twitch as if the hunter had just spotted his prey.

THE BOSS

The other; the other.

He runs the back of his right hand down the length of Dee's upper arm.

THE BOSS

The other was your beauty.

Still with his sweet tone, laced with the ravenous hunger, he whispers into her ear.

THE BOSS

Understand this. You will be thrown in with all the other losers here if you fail me.

Dispatcher (Dee) refuses to make eye contact.

She speaks with an oppressed, nearly trapped voice.

DISPATCHER (DEE)
I understand. May I go now?

Dee stands and turns from him, but is still within reach - although not being physically touched, she cringes.

Talking just above a whisper, he speaks with an expression of near ecstasy.

THE BOSS
You may go. But don't consider playing any more games with me.

He smiles and tilts his head slightly to the right.

THE BOSS
I have many spies. Some of them will be watching you very closely.

Dee responds with the same trapped, oppressed voice.

DEE
Yes, I know.

She cringes again, but still not being touched by her boss.

DEE
With your leave, my lord Satan.

Dee opens the office door. As she does, the screams and cries greatly increase in volume. She walks out of the office and into the swirling smoke.

CUT TO:

EXT. A DARK, OVERCAST DAY - OPEN, DUSTY LANDSCAPE WITH NO TREES IN SIGHT. THERE'S A LARGE HILL IN THE CENTER OF THE PICTURE. THE SHOT SLOWLY MOVES TOWARDS THE CENTER OF THE HILL. THERE ARE PEOPLE MULLING AROUND IN THE SCENE. THEIR DRESS AND THE LOOK OF THE SETTING PLACES THE SCENE IN ANCIENT ISRAEL - ABOUT 32 AD.

The shot progresses to the center of the hill. As the view on the hill becomes clear, there are three men on three crosses, each man dead. She is speaking with sadness and remorse.

> DEE (VO)
> It was that day on Skull Mountain. The Israelites called it Golgotha Hill.

The shot stops and focuses on the cross in the center. The dead body of Jesus hangs motionless.

> DEE (VO)
> That was the day that my whole outlook changed. The events of that week were on my list.

Dee's voice is remorseful, yet she speaks as a lieutenant reporting to her captain of the success of her mission.

> DEE (VO)
> I pushed at the people around him. I whispered into their ears the things I wanted them to say. Through those fools, I succeeded in the biggest mission I'd ever been assigned.

All the while, the scene is still looking at Jesus hanging on the cross.

> DEE (VO)
>
> My boss was so-very-pleased with me. He gave me the next earth- year off to play. I didn't feel much like playing.

Dee's voice cracks as she nearly cries.

> DEE (VO)
>
> The man on the cross cried out, 'Forgive them; forgive them.' We killed him and his last words were for us to be forgiven?

The shot moves closer to Jesus centering on his face and head.

Dee's voice is slightly more controlled.

> DEE (VO)
>
> After that, I couldn't bring myself to be involved with such outright evil ever again.

The scene grows hazy and begins to fade.

She speaks with overwhelming sadness.

> DEE (VO)
>
> I cried for months. I ran even longer - from the memory of that day.

The scene is more hazy now, but still identifiable.

Dee's voice becomes closer to normal. She speaks as with a newfound determination.

> DEE (VO)
>
> Then I got the idea of how I could try to make up for some the evil I'd perpetrated over the years.

The scene fades completely.

CUT TO:

EXT. A CHILLY, SNOW COVERED COUNTRYSIDE DEVOID OF BUILDINGS WITH A NARROW, SLIGHTLY SNOW COVERED DIRT ROAD CURVING THROUGH IT. WINTER - EARLY 1945 - GERMANY.

There are four black, early 1940s, European four-door sedans in a speeding caravan on the road.

Dee is speaking with a clear voice that seems to be growing in confidence.

DEE (VO)
Before the end of my year off, I came to a dangerous decision. I decided that I'd continue to take my assignments from the boss as I had for centuries. But -

The four black cars are moving quickly down the dirt road sliding a little on the snowy road.

DEE (VO)
Instead of following them to the letter, I'd come up with a way for the people I encountered to escape the evil that the list contained.

As Dee talks, we move closer to the second car in the caravan.

DEE (VO)
Each situation was different. Each improvisation was a gamble.

The shot moves to the second moving car and aims at the rear passenger window.

> DEE (VO)
> Like the time Hitler was on his way to the airport. He was traveling in his car with one of his top advisors.

> CUT TO:

INT.- INSIDE THE SECOND SEDAN. TWO GERMANS IN UNIFORM. ONE SOLDIER DRIVING WITH ONE OFFICER IN THE FRONT PASSENGER SEAT TURNED WITH HIS TOTAL ATTENTION BEING GIVEN TO THE PASSENGER. THE LONE PASSENGER IN THE REAR SEAT IS HITLER. HE IS WEARING A WARM OVERCOAT AND HAS AN ANGRY AND IMPATIENT LOOK ABOUT HIM.

The snowy, wooded countryside can be seen flying by through the car windows.

> GERMAN OFFICER
> Mine Fuhrer, we should be at the airport within the hour.

Hitler speaks with insolence and anger.

> HITLER
> We had better be. I have waited long enough to force this world to submit to my reign.

Hitler looks at the closed packet of papers he's holding in his left hand. The officer is hanging onto every word that Hitler speaks.

His voice moves from insolence to arrogance, but still is laced with barely controlled anger.

                    HITLER

The information that this envelope contains is of just the right magnitude to generate a controlled global catastrophe greater than this world has ever known.

Hitler looks out the window. Following a short pause, he continues.

                    HITLER

Germany will sweep powerfully across the lands and subdue this entire planet before any country can recover.

EXT. THE VIEW IS OF THE BLACK SEDANS MOVING ALONG THE SNOWY, DIRT ROAD. THE VIEW IS JUST FAR ENOUGH AWAY TO SEE ALL FOUR CARS.

The cars are still speeding along the road. A snowy cloud is flying up from the cars so the rear sedan is barely visible.

Dee speaks confidently as one enacting a plan.

                    DEE (VO)

I'd found the line of cars traveling along the snowy, dirt road towards the airport. My assignment was to protect the Fuhrer's caravan from the Allied Forces stationed at several points along the route.

The view is moving towards Hitler's car window again.

Still confidant.

                    DEE (VO)

To make it appear I'd completed my assignment, I disabled several of the vehicles within the Allied units that were stationed along the trail. It rendered them harmless to Hitler's caravan.

The view is now about to enter Hitler's window again.

Dee voice now contains a slowly growing determination.

DEE (VO)
Now, it was time to address Hitler.

INT. INSIDE HITLER'S SEDAN, HE IS NOW REVIEWING THE PAPERS, OCCASIONALLY LOOKING OUT THE SIDE WINDOW, SHAKING HIS HEAD AND RETURNING TO READING THE PAPERS. THE SNOWY COUNTRYSIDE BEING PASSED BY IS SEEN THROUGH THE WINDOWS OF THE SEDAN.

Dee speaks with confidence and determination.

DEE (VO)
In an hour, the scientists that the German leader is counting on will be assisted out of the country and into Canada by the United States government.

Hitler checks his pocket watch.

DEE (VO)
If captured, the work the scientists have completed in creating the Atomic Bomb will go to the Fuhrer. He could then force the completion of the bomb's development and move to conquer the world.

Hitler is slowly shaking his head.

DEE (VO)

With the Allies out of the way, the scientists would arrive at the airport at the same time as the Fuhrer - as long as his journey remains uninterrupted.

Hitler speaks with a visible anger.

HITLER

Driver, go faster. The airplane will not wait.

The driver replies with obvious fear in his voice.

GERMAN DRIVER

Yes, mine Fuhrer.

Hitler speaks to himself proudly.

HITLER

With this bomb, I can detonate it over the capitol of each of our enemies.

Hitler slowly throws his shoulders back and straightens as if he were sitting at attention. He turns his head slightly and appears to look down his nose while speaking.

HITLER

That will surely cause them to listen to the words that will come from their new Fatherland. The words that will come from their Fuhrer.

EXT. THE CARS CONTINUE TO SPEED ALONG THE SNOWY, DIRT ROAD.

DEE (VO)

Hitler's plan to drop that many bombs all over the Earth would not result in global domination. His plans would instead result in global destruction.

Her voice pauses as the cars continue on their journey. She then speaks with determination.

> DEE (VO)
>
> I couldn't let that happen. I had to come up with a plan - some way to stop the Fuhrer while at the same time not get caught disobeying my boss's direct orders.

EXT. - THE VIEW MOVES AWAY FROM THE CARS AND TRAVELS ABOUT TWO MILES AHEAD OF THE CARAVAN WHILE SLOWLY SWEEPING THE SURROUNDING COUNTRYSIDE. IT'S A ROLLING, WOODED, SNOW COVERED COUNTRYSIDE.

Dee speaks with the confidence of just coming up with an idea.

> DEE (VO)
>
> I decided to find the spies that were following me. The same minions that've followed me for over a hundred years.

EXT. THE SCENE SETTLES ON A ROCK FORMATION JUST TO THE SIDE OF THE ROAD ABOUT FIFTY FEET FROM THE EDGE OF THE ROAD - STILL TWO MILES AHEAD OF HITLER'S CARAVAN.

Four oddly dressed, somewhat deformed, human-looking creatures are seen behind a rock formation along the side of the snow covered road. They seem to be giggling to each other as if they knew something that no one else knew. One look at them, and you were sure that wasn't possible.

> DEE (VO)
>
> Normally, my form is very human. That's also true with the forms of the sub-demons that follow me.

The four little creatures are still giggling and appear to be playing a game of touch and keep-away with each other.

DEE (VO)
I usually appear to be a tall brunette with a slight streak of blonde just above my forehead.

The view is moving closer to the spot of the four demons.

DEE (VO)
This shape helps me be accepted in almost any situation and it's the only form that these moron sub-demons know me by.

The view is very close to the four creatures. Dee is invisible and is getting closer to the four demons, but not yet making a sound.

DEE (VO)
My plan was to change into a form most hated by the sub-demons - an Angel. They can't stand Angels. In fact, each time they see an Angel, their anger rages and they seem to become more stupid than they usually are.

Dee is now visible and standing at the top of the hill dressed in a white, flowing, one-piece garment that gives her the basic look of an angel. There are no wings.

DEE (VO)
Shortly after I located the four sub-demons behind a small rock formation along the road, I transformed into the form of an Angel. To the humans, we're still invisible; but, we can see one another quite clearly.

Dee directs herself to the foursome. She speaks to them as if she were tempting children with candy.

DEE

Hey Bone.

DEE (VO)

He's the leader of the four sub-demons.

One of the demons begins looking around to find who has called out his name.

DEE (VO)

The other three have similarly intelligent names - Bobble, Dog and Slug. They seemed to be very happy about it when they were given these names, so they never changed them.

Dee calls out to the leader again - still in a voice of tempting children with candy.

DEE

Bone, what are you and your goblins doing in Germany? Did you lose your way home?

The foursome now see Dee at the top of the hill. They take on a look of anger and excitement as they immediately respond to Dee's taunting.

ALL FOUR DEMONS

Eerrr, eerrr.

DEE (VO)

They were never able to talk. They just grunt and growl.

Dee taunts them again. Her looking like an angel did seem to get their attention very quickly.

132

DEE

Come get me you fools, if you can?

Dee starts running down the hill at a slight angle with the snow-covered road. The four sub-demons following close behind. All the while, they continue to grunt and make noises.

ALL FOUR DEMONS

Uugghh, rollff, eerrr.

DEE (VO)

Sub-demons, in their human form, are quite squat.

The foursome begins to pick up velocity and excitement in their race to catch an angel.

DEE (VO)

They're no more than five feet tall, poorly coordinated, but with the strength of ten humans each.

The demons were now frothing at the mouth with anticipation.

ALL FOUR DEMONS

Uugghh, rollff, eerrr.

DEE (VO)

I was trying to capitalize on this combination of unusual characteristics.

The four demons are chasing Dee down the sloping, snowy hillside with Dee still appearing as an angel. They are all moving just above the snow, leaving no tracks in the snow.

> DEE (VO)
>
> They were following very close - as close as I'd let them. I was hoping that they'd stay so close they couldn't watch where they were going. Blinded by their anger, all they could see in front of them was me.

Dee turned to look back at them and saw that they were all drooling and that Bone was grinning like a cat about to catch a mouse. The four of them thought today would be the day they would catch an Angel.

Dee taunted them again.

> DEE
>
> Pay attention boys. I wouldn't want you to lose sight of me.

> ALL FOUR DEMONS
>
> Roarerer.

Dee speaks with a chuckle in her voice.

> DEE (VO)
>
> I just love messin' with these guys.

The chase is very close. The four demons seem to be closing on Dee. Dee turns suddenly and is now running directly towards the snow-covered road.

> DEE (VO)
>
> I was almost at my destination with the four of them right behind me.

The chase is nearing the road with the four sub-demons nearly within reach of Dee.

DEE (VO)

Of course, no one in the caravan could see any of this chase. We physically exist, but still invisible to humans.

With one sharp upward pull, Dee shot into the air.

DEE (VO)

Just as I'd hoped, those short little misfits couldn't react that quickly.

With the force of four rushing torpedoes, they each hit one of the four cars traveling in the Fuhrer's caravan. The impact of the charging, muscular numbskulls, was enough to cause the cars to tumble from the snowy road and onto their sides into the snow-covered countryside.

DEE (VO)

Hitler's cars would go no further today.

The impact also left the four little mounds of demonic ignorance scattered unconscious along the snowy road. Dee stands at the top of the hillside that overlooks the entire scene and laughs.

DEE (VO)

I not only was able to stop the Fuhrer from his plan of world domination.

Dee speaks with a laugh.

DEE (VO)

But I'd once again pulled the wool over the eyes of Bone, Bobble, Dog and Slug.

CUT TO:

INT, CIVIL WAR YEARS -- RICHMOND, IN. -- LATE NIGHT. SMALL, BUT NEATLY KEPT HOUSE. A KIND LOOKING MAN, DARK, FULL HEAD OF HAIR, MID-THIRTIES, WARM EYES, WITH AN EARNESTLY CONCERNED LOOK ON HIS FACE. HE'S SITTING WITH DEE AT A RECTANGULAR, WOODEN, KITCHEN TABLE WITH A SINGLE OIL-BURNING LAMP GLOWING IN THE CENTER OF THE TABLE.

Dee and the man are talking intently with each other.

> DEE (VO)
> What an existence this has been. So many **assignments** are given each day to so many demons.

The view of the two talking to each other is seen slowly from all around their position.

> DEE (VO)
> I've been able to disobey orders for a long time. But I wasn't sure how long I'd be able to keep it up. I knew when I was discovered, I'd be thrown into the pit for eternity.

The view is centering on the two of them again, sitting at the kitchen table.

> DEE (VO)
> I've known that from the start though. But the good I've been trying to doing is more important than what my eternal existence was ever meant to be.

The view is now only the man. He's listening to Dee.

DEE (VO)

There was a man, Milton Wright, that I'd shared my secret with during America's Civil War. He was a good man who later in his life served as a Bishop of the United Brethren Church for nearly fifty years.

Their conversation is very animated. Dee first has her hands waving as she talks and then the man has his moving as he talks.

MILTON

So you were there at the crucifixion of our Christ?

DEE

I was there all right. I even held the bowl where Pilot washed his hands.

MILTON

Oh, this is very hard to believe. And you were there when Jesus was hung on the cross?

DEE

I handed the guard the nails.

DEE (VO)

The conversations would sometimes go on for hours. Milton's questions hammered home all the evil I'd perpetrated; yet he grew more fascinated with each story I shared.

DEE (VO)

Milton was a young man when I first met him. Just married. He and his wife had no children yet but they planned to when the war was over. He was a very caring man. He listened to my entire story.

The two are shown continuing in an active, animated conversation.

The man speaks with a convinced tone as if he had just won a debate.

MILTON

This is proof that God has and apparently always will work in mysterious ways.

DEE (VO)

I never felt worthy of Milton's assessment, or his friendship. He spoke with me as if I were his friend and not a high-ranking demon.

The view gently backs away from the kitchen table.

CUT TO:

EXT. NIGHT - MILTON AND FOUR OTHERS STAND QUIETLY ALONG A DARK, WOODED RIVERBANK. THEY HAVE ONLY A SINGLE OIL LAMP BETWEEN THEM. SACKS OF FOOD, CANTEENS FILLED WITH FRESH WATER, CLOTHES AND BLANKETS SIT IN THE MIDDLE OF THE GROUP. THEY'RE ALL LOOKING OUT ACROSS THE RIVER.

DEE (VO)

Milton's church was located in Richmond, Indiana, a safe distance from the southern border of Indiana. They provided a safe house for runaway slaves to rest in before going further north. Whenever possible, I'd inform my friend Milton of escaped slaves that were trying to flee to the northern states searching for freedom. One time in particular I told him of two groups I'd heard about trying to leave Kentucky. These slaves had all been part of one group until half of them had been sold. The sale had split up a husband and wife, Moses and Lila.

Milton and the others are looking towards the river, occasionally looking up and down the riverbank.

DEE (VO)

At times, Milton would accompany a few of his closest friends and travel to the Kentucky / Indiana state line personally to transport the runaways to Richmond. This was one of those nights.

One of Milton's group had rowed across the river and tied a rope off on the other side. Leaving two of the group on the Kentucky side to help load the boat, they sent the first load of slaves across on the flat bottom riverboat.

A small group of runaway Slaves come slowly out of the water and are met with dry blankets by Milton's group.

I had asked Milton if I could come along on this evening's effort.

MILTON

Of course; but why tonight?

DEE

I've got a feeling this is one of those special times that my boss would like to intervene. If I'm there, maybe I see it coming before any trouble starts.

The night was overcast and pitch black, and except for the single oil lamp on either side of the river, there was no light.

Dee had taken the form of a man and was dressed much the same as the rest of the group.

MILTON

This is my friend Dee, from the Deep South. He's a sympathizer with our cause. I thought we could use the extra help tonight.

DEE (VO)

Milton's other friends shook my hand and accepted me without question. I was Milton's friend, that's all that mattered.

MILTON

Dee, let's you and I take the boat back over this time. Moses and Lila should be ready for the next trip.

DEE (VO)

Milton and I boarded the riverboat and began pulling the rope hand over hand until we arrived at the riverbank on the other side.

The boat pushes against the muddy riverbank on the Kentucky side of the river. As it does, four runaways come from the darkness to the boat. The first two are elderly gentlemen. Dee, who is sitting in the end of the boat furthest from the bank, helps them sit without jarring the boat too much.

The last two are a man and a woman. Moses and Lila. Milton turns his head as if he's heard something from the darkness.

MILTON

We must hurry my friends, I believe someone is coming.

Milton takes Moses by the hand and pulls him into the boat, then turns to take the hand of the waiting Lila.

DEE (VO)

That's when I heard the dogs. They were close - very close.

DEE

Hurry it up folks. We're out of time.

MILTON

Start pulling the rope. Pull now!

No sooner had Milton said those words when all hell broke loose. Milton had Lila by the hand as the dogs rushed from the darkness and toppled Lila into the water. It was so dark no one in the front of the boat, including Moses, could see what was happening.

MILTON

Oh dear God! Pull folks, pull! Your lives depend upon it!

DEE (VO)

But I could see what was going on. Four dogs had been loosed by their owners, the slave hunters, just now in sight on the riverbank. The dogs had rushed at Lila in a death frenzy, following the lead dog into the water. The dogs snapped and clawed at Lila pushing her head below the water in the first moment of their attack. She never made a sound.

MILTON

Pull, I tell you, pull!

DEE (VO)

A shiver went through me as the dogs finished with Lila. Her body now floated face down in the water and the dogs were retreating for the shore. The lead dog turned and looked straight at me, his eyes locking with mine. It was Bone! The dog smiled. I knew he couldn't recognize me. He was just smiling at whoever was looking.

The boat made it to the Indiana shore and ran up into the mud.

MOSES

We made it Lila! We made it!

Moses turned, for the first time, away from the rope-pull.

MOSES

Lila? Where's my Lila?

MILTON

She's gone, my friend. She's gone.

MOSES

No, she can't be...

Moses races into the water only to be stopped by Milton and two of the others.

MOSES

This was supposed to be freedom for both of us - both of us. We'll go back for her.

MILTON

Lila was killed by those bastard dogs from hell. She's with the Father now my son. She's with the Father.

Moses came back out of the water with the others. Sobbing, he said,

MOSES

Must move on. I'll cry for my Lila when we all is safe. No time for tears now.

On the journey back, Dee and Milton are riding together in the front of the lead wagon.

MILTON

I heard the dogs, but they moved so fast. Faster than any dogs I've ever seen.

DEE

They were bastards from hell, like you said.

MILTON

What do you mean Dee?

DEE

I knew them. They were sub-demons in the form of dogs.

MILTON

You knew? And you did nothing about it?

DEE

What could I do? They were on that slave so fast. She was as good as dead when she hit the water.

MILTON

That slave was a woman. And that woman's name was Lila. And yes, she's dead, no thanks to you. Or were you here to make sure that she did die?

                    DEE

What are you saying? Do you think I led you here
to watch her die?

                  MILTON

It's what you do, isn't it? It's what you were created
for - death and destruction for all humanity. Isn't
that right? Well isn't it?

                    DEE

Yes, Milton. It is exactly what I was created to do.
But I had nothing to do with what went on here
tonight.

                  MILTON

Nothing is right. You just sat there, knowing that the
dogs were other demons, and watched that poor
girl die a horrible death.

They were both silent for a few moments. Dee broke the
silence.

                    DEE

If I'd made a move to help her, then Satan would
know about me for sure. I would have been cast
into the pit of Hell for all eternity.

They both rode silently along for several moments.

Milton speaks with a sad, distant resolve.

                  MILTON

If I'd jumped into the water to help, the dogs of Hell
would have surely killed me as well.

He pauses, then continues.

MILTON

Until you and I have come to terms with our missions, we'll be of no real help to anyone. We are both too fearful to offer our lives for the sake of another. Lila's death is proof of that.

DEE

Milton, you were--

MILTON

No. I was cowardly. You too were cowardly. And as a result of our mutual cowardice, a young woman is dead.

The rest of the trip was silent. No words were spoken until their return to Richmond.

EXT. OUTSIDE OF MILTON'S HOUSE - DARK, JUST BEFORE DAWN - A CLEAR NIGHT. THE WAGON IS PARKED TO THE SIDE OF THE HOUSE AND DEE AND MILTON ARE STANDING ALONE IN THE FRONT YARD OF THE HOUSE.

MILTON

I thank you Dee for your help this evening. I do look forward to your next visit. Maybe you should plan on that visit in a few months or so, to give us both time.

DEE (VO)

His words hurt. But the hurt I felt for the loss of Lila was far greater.

Dee pauses.

>   DEE (VO)
> I waited six months before I visited Milton again.
> We never spoke of that evening again.

>   CUT TO:

INT. BACK IN MILTON'S HOUSE. EARLY EVENING, THE
HOUSE IS WELL LIGHTED WITH OIL LAMPS. MILTON
AND HIS WIFE ARE IN THE KITCHEN WITH TWO
YOUNG CHILDREN WHO LOOK TO BE TODDLERS.

He and his wife are bathing their two sons in a round,
metal washtub in the kitchen.

>   DEE (VO)
> Milton survived the war and became a father to his
> first son during the year of 1867.

Milton and his wife continue bathing the boys, obviously
enjoying the effort. They are making loving gestures
and making little loving comments to each other and to
the boys.

>   DEE (VO)
> Their second son was born in 1871. Milton and his
> wife raised their two sons, Orville and Wilbur, to
> be kind, inquisitive and innovative.

INT. BACK IN THE BOSS'S OFFICE. THE BOSS IS
WALKING AWAY FROM DEE AND PREPARING TO SIT
IN HIS HIGH-BACKED, RED LEATHER CHAIR.

The Boss has just handed Dee a list of new assignments.

>   DEE (VO)
> It was on a morning in the year of 1900 that I
> received my list of orders from the boss. At the very

top of the list were Wilbur and Orville's names, but the names had lines drawn through them.

Sitting in the low-backed, red leather chair, Dee cautiously addresses her Boss.

DEE

Excuse me Sir, but why are these names marked out?

The Boss replies with a calm yet indignant tone.

THE BOSS

It's really none of your business. But it could be a lot of fun for some of your coworkers, so I'll tell you.

The Boss smiles broadly as he speaks with a tone that seems to deeply relish every word that comes out of his own mouth.

THE BOSS

I had originally assigned this project to you, but I changed my mind. I gave the assignment to Bone, Bobble, Dog and Slug. The look of excitement on their grotesque faces made my day.

Dee was still pushing to discover what was planned for the sons of her, long-time friend.

DEE

Yes Sir, but what's the assignment?

He speaks with an obviously unsatisfied hunger in his voice.

THE BOSS

They are going to make sure that when these two attempt flight, something goes wrong causing at

147

least one of them to die - preferably Orville since he's currently expected to live much longer than his brother.

The Boss sits slowly in his chair as if he wanted to pleasurably take in every element of the moment.

> THE BOSS
> I don't care about when these earthlings succeed in flying.

He looks out through the office window to the smoke-filled surroundings.

> THE BOSS
> It's their father I'm after. Their father was a great enemy of mine during their Civil War. I was never able to get at him - then. But I intend to get to him now, through his sons.

Dee hurriedly stands.

> DEE
> I have to be going Sir. I have a lot of work to do if I hope to complete my orders as listed.

The Boss turns to Dee and nearly growls as he speaks.

> THE BOSS
> Complete the list or you know what the consequence will be!

CUT TO:

EXT. OUTSIDE—DAYTIME—A ROLLING HILLSIDE IN THE BACKGROUND WITH A LARGE HILL OFF TO THE LEFT

AND AN EXPANSIVE, FLAT FIELD STRETCHING TO THE RIGHT OF THE HILL FOR AT LEAST A MILE.

DEE (VO)
I left there as fast as I could and traveled to the place where I was sure to find Wilbur and Orville.

EXT. AT THE TOP OF THE HILL, TWO MEN ARE MAKING ADJUSTMENTS ON WHAT LOOKS LIKE A MOTORIZED BICYCLE WITH WINGS, WHILE A SMALL GROUP OF PEOPLE STAND A SHORT DISTANCE AWAY.

DEE (VO)
Today's the day they'd attempt to glide their small, motorized glider down the side of a hill near Kitty Hawk.

Dee's view is from the sky. The view changes as she comes to the ground to the east of the hill and apparently lands.

DEE
The name of the hill couldn't be more gruesome. It's called Kill Devil Hill. Somehow I had to find a way to protect the sons of the only friend I'd ever known.

The two men continue to make adjustments to the machine. They are speaking to one another, but we cannot hear the content of their conversation.

DEE (VO)
I searched for the four sub-demons in order to spy on them in hopes of discovering their plans.

Dee walks towards the hill from the west.

> DEE
>
> They're always easy to find when they're on assignment. All I have to do is locate the general area, sit and listen.

Dee sits quietly on the ground.

> DEE (VO)
>
> They get so excited on an assignment that they can't stop giggling and howling just thinking about how they're going to destroy someone.

On the ground, just to the East of the hill, Dee has her legs folded with her hands resting on her knees.

> DEE (VO)
>
> I sat near Kill Devil Hill for nearly an hour listening for their unmistakable noises.

EXT. SOUNDS OF THE FOUR DEMONS GROWLING CAN BE HEARD FAINTLY IN THE BACKGROUND.

Dee sounds as if she is calming a bit since discovering the whereabouts of the four sub-demons.

> DEE (VO)
>
> At last, I heard them growling from the other side of the hill.

Dee began moving in the direction of the noises.

> DEE (VO)
>
> I stayed invisible as I gained a vantage to spy on them.

EXT. A SMALL GATHERING OF GEESE ARE MULLING AROUND A RECENTLY WORKED FIELD. THEY ARE

GATHERING IN THE AREA THAT DEE HEARD THE
SOUNDS FROM THE SUB-DEMONS.

> DEE (VO)
> They had changed their forms to look like geese
> and were mingling with a gaggle of real geese.

The four sub-demons look like awkward, only slightly
larger than normal geese as they walk around within the
gaggle of real geese.

Dee has a calm, confident tone to her voice now.

> DEE (VO)
> When I saw them, their plan became clear to me.

Dee stood and moved closer to the gaggle of geese.

> DEE (VO)
> They were planning to wait until a specific flight
> attempt had commenced. They then would lead the
> real geese and fly them directly into the path of
> the glider causing its pilot to lose control and crash.
> I needed to stop this. Somehow, stop them from
> guiding the geese into the flight path of the glider.

Dee sat down very near the geese, still invisible to the
four demons.

> DEE (VO)
> I decided to wait until I saw the four growling
> goons make their move. Then I'd make mine. They'd
> waited until the twelfth attempt by the two brothers
> to glide down the mountain because they wanted
> to kill Orville instead of Wilbur. This was Orville's
> first attempt.

Most of the geese are calmly lying around while a few are moving gently amongst the others.

> DEE (VO)
> They were certain that killing Orville would be most pleasing to their boss. They always were such 'red-nosers' with the boss.

EXT. THE TWO MEN AND A FEW OF THEIR ASSISTANTS WERE AT THE TOP OF THE HILL READYING THE GLIDER FOR ANOTHER ATTEMPT AT FLIGHT. ORVILLE WRIGHT WAS AT THE CONTROLS OF THE GLIDER.

> DEE (VO)
> Orville was at the top of the hill ready to push off while Bone and his goons, looking like clumsy geese in the middle of the real gaggle of geese, were waiting on the backside of the hill. Orville pushed off from the top of the hill.

The glider lifts off from the ground and takes flight.

> DEE (VO)
> Bone stirred up the geese and they began to head straight for the glider's path.

The geese are flying right at the glider from its left side. Orville Wright does not yet notice the gaggle.

> DEE (VO)
> At a point where the geese, real and demonic, were still about fifty feet from the glider, I flew into the sky disguised as my boss and hovered, midair, between the geese and the glider.

Dee is suspended in the air between the glider and the flying gaggle. She appears as The Boss.

Dee shouts at the four minions.

                    DEE
    You fools! What do you think you're doing?

The four demons, bunched up in the gaggle of geese,
are shocked by the immediate sight of their boss.

              ALL FOUR DEMONS
    Ahh? Eerruh?

                  DEE (VO)
    My ploy was working. There's something very
    consistent with all sub-demons.

The four demons lose their control on their forms as
geese and return to their demonic forms.

                  DEE (VO)
    They've gotta concentrate really hard in order to
    maintain any form other than their own.

There is a pronounced look of shock and surprise on the
four sub-demon's faces.

                  DEE (VO)
    Need I say more? With their concentration broken,
    they changed back to their own form and began
    to fall to the ground.

The four demons seem suspended for a brief moment
before plummeting to the ground.

                  DEE (VO)
    This broke up the real geese who flew off in the
    opposite direction squawking and croaking all the

way. Those sub-demons; they fall really well, but they don't land with much style.

The demons hit the earth's surface so hard they leave holes in the ground three feet deep and just lay there stunned, unable to move.

Orville landed without mishap.

Dee's voice is heard in peaceful tones.

DEE (VO)
The sons of Milton Wright were now free to continue their research unencumbered by the gruesome foursome.

CUT TO:

Aerial view of approaching a major city. Slowly getting closer and closer to the city, and then continuing on into the city. This view continues during Dee's voice over until she is standing in a high-rise apartment, one of the upper floors, in front of an apartment door.

DEE (VO)
As the years went by, it had become more and more difficult to sabotage my orders. I could always rely on the ineptitude of my co-workers. There was this once though I had to rely on someone far greater than me.

It was an assignment like any other. I had been given a new list or orders and the first on the list was for me to pose as a baby sitter for a ten-year-old girl. She was a cute little thing who had never hurt a soul. She was on my list because her mother and father were about to get a divorce. Not only that, but her mother and father had been arguing for some time about all kinds of things; so much so, they had said more than once the only reason they were still together was because of the little girl.

The mother and father both worked and were in the habit of taking the little girl to their sitter's house they had used for years. This morning though, they had received a call from the sitter saying she had fallen down and possibly broken her leg so she could not sit for the girl today. My boss is very thorough.

Anyway, I had placed my telephone number on the neighborhood information board at the local grocery store and the girl's mother had found the number. I arrived at their apartment located on the sixteenth floor of an inner-city high rise.

DEE
"Hello. You called me as a replacement sitter for the day."

Kelly's Mom
"Yes, come in. There's plenty of food in the refrigerator. Kelly has plenty of games in her room she plays with and any of her friends are welcome to come over if they call. I wish I didn't have to rush off like this; but, I'm already late for work as it is. Kelly, dear, I'm leaving."

Little Kelly comes walking slowly from her room balancing herself on her crutches, with both legs in metal braces.

DEE (VO)
Kelly had practically no control over her legs since birth and would more than likely never recover.

Kelly
"You have a good day Mama. I'll be fine."

Kelly's Mom
"You just be yourself and I'll be very proud of you baby."

DEE
"We'll be fine Mrs. Johnson. Don't worry about us."

Dee and Kelly are sitting in the living room watching TV. The coffee table has a couple of board game boxes siting on it.

DEE (VO)
I was worried enough for the both of us. I had just finished a meeting with my boss and he was not sympathetic at all with my reasons for failing on my recent assignments. He told me he was losing his patience with me all together. Patience had never been one of his vices.

Kelly's mother left for work and my day with the little girl began. We played games, talked and watched TV for a while before it was time for her afternoon nap. I had dreaded this naptime since the moment I had received my new orders. It was during this nap I was to set fire to the apartment so this lovely little girl would have no chance to escape.

Before she went to sleep, I sat with her for a minute to talk.

DEE
"You're a very sweet little girl Kelly."

Kelly

"Thank you Miss Dee. I like you too."

DEE

"Kelly, do you believe in God?"

Kelly

"Oh yes. I say my prayers every night asking for God to do something to help my mother and father fall in love again so they can be happy together."

DEE

"Do you ever ask God to help you?"

Kelly

"Not often. I don't believe God is hard of hearing. So, if I have asked Him once to fix my legs then I am sure he has heard me."

DEE

"I'm sure that's very true Kelly, but will you do me a favor this one time?"

Kelly

"Sure. What's the favor?"

DEE

"Will you say your prayers before your nap and ask God again to heal your legs?"

Kelly

"Sure. I never get tired of talking to God. Can I ask God to bless you also Miss Dee?"

DEE (VO)

This was the most beautiful soul I had ever met.

DEE

"Of course, and thank you dear."

Kelly knelt down at the side of her little bed and silently prayed. The only word she said out loud was "Amen" at the end of her prayer.

DEE

"There's a good little girl. Now you lay down and think about your prayer while you are falling to sleep."

Dee is walking away from the bed Kelly is now napping in. Dee is seen pouring water on the apartment carpet from the bedroom to the front door as the voice over continues.

DEE (VO)

I walked away from the little girl feeling so helpless. Demons had long ago lost the right to pray to God, so all I could do was hope. I sat in the living room for over an hour before I caused the furnace to break apart at the seams and engulf the surrounding closet area in flames. I had treated the carpet that went from the edge of the little girl's bed to the front door of the apartment with water just in case she awoke from the smoke and might then be able to escape.

Dee sits on the floor with her back against the far wall.

DEE (VO)

I now sat in the comer of the bedroom looking at the little girl while I cried. I was ordered to stay until, well, until it was over to make sure I didn't mess this one up. The flames were all over the apartment now and there wasn't much hope of this cute little girl waking up. Even if she did, with her crippled legs, she would still be trapped.

A blue-white glow came into the girl's room and surrounded her bed

DEE (VO)
I had never seen anything like this light before. The color was so soft it appeared to be full of peace and enriched with love.

Kelly began to awaken coughing from the smoke. She saw the flames and jumped from her bed with the legs of an athlete. She paused and looked at her legs while moving her hands slowly down them feeling their strength.

Kelly
"Miss Dee! Miss Dee! The apartment is on fire!"

DEE (VO)
She could not see me. I had been invisible in the comer of her room and was all too surprised by the vision I saw to make myself visible.

Kelly
"I hope she is already out of the building! I've got to get out of here!"

With these words, Kelly runs across the water soaked floor and from the blazing apartment into the hallway and down the steps to the street. As Kelly comes running from the front entrance of the apartment building, she sees her mother and father being prevented by the firemen from entering the burning building to save their little girl.

Kelly

"Mama! Daddy! I'm all right! Look, my legs are healed! I can run!"

DEE (VO)

I looked down into the street from the window of the burning apartment to see the three of them hugging more strongly than they ever had. I was still crying, but these were tears of happiness. That's when I heard a strange noise coming from the little girl's now engulfed room. To this day, I'm sure I heard, "Thank you Dispatcher."

CUT TO:

INT. MODERN DAY - HIGH SCHOOL CLASSROOM - MIDWEST - FORT WAYNE, IN. THE STUDENTS ARE JUST COMING INTO THE ROOM FOR THE START OF CLASS. THERE IS A MIXTURE OF GIRLS AND BOYS - ABOUT THIRTY IN ALL.

DEE (VO)

Not long ago, I was sent on another troubling assignment. On this assignment, I had to pose as a younger version of myself - a high school student.

Dee walks into the classroom. She looks as Dee always has, but with skin-tone and hair cut differences that give her the look of a fifteen-year-old girl. She sits at a desk in the rear of the classroom.

DEE (VO)

There was this boy. Basically a good kid, but he was new at the school and was finding it easier to get accepted by the group who was nearly always in trouble.

A teenage boy now enters the classroom. He's tall for his age, about six feet and has a sturdy, almost muscular body weighing between one hundred and fifty to one hundred seventy pounds.

He sits in the rear of the class as well.

> DEE (VO)
> His name is Joshua. Everyone calls him Josh. He was my new assignment.

The teacher steps into the classroom.

> TEACHER
> Good morning class. Let's get settled - everyone find a seat.

> DEE (VO)
> He had some problems. I was sent to give him a few more.

The teacher is reading through a roll call trying to be as informal as she can by just calling out each student's first name while Dee is speaking above the action.

> DEE (VO)
> Josh was going to face some decisions soon and I was supposed to befriend him and guide him towards the wrong choices.

> TEACHER
> Josh.

> JOSH
> Here.

TEACHER

Josh, aren't you from Southside?

JOSH

I went there through last year.

Me and my mom moved over the summer. Were close to here now.

TEACHER

I thought so. I helped out for a few weeks at Southside last year. I think you were in my class there. Good to have you with us this year.

The other students had been ignoring the conversation between Josh and the teacher. Except for Dee.

TEACHER

Dee.

DEE

Here.

TEACHER

You're new this year as well. Where were you last year?

DEE

Last year I was in Texas. The year before that I was in California. The year before, well my family moves around a lot.

TEACHER

It sounds like it. I hope your stay here is a good one. Do you think you'll get to stay here for a while?

                    DEE

I doubt it.

The teacher moves on to start discussing the text books and how the homework will be assigned.

Dee whispers to Josh.

                    DEE

Hi, I'm Dee.

                    JOSH

I know. I just heard.

                    DEE

Guess ya did.

Josh pulled back and sat low in his chair as if he were trying to disappear.

                  DEE (VO)
I decided to try to talk with Josh again after class.

The bell next to the classroom clock rings and the students begin standing to leave the room.

                    DEE
Do you know the way to the cafeteria? This is my first day and I'm a little lost.

                    JOSH
You can walk with me if you'd like. I'm going to lunch this period too.

DEE (VO)

I walked a little behind Josh as he led the way to the lunchroom. He walked fast. I had to work a little to keep up.

JOSH

Here it is. I usually sit along the right wall. There's almost always seats open over there if you want to sit there.

DEE

Thanks. I'd like to.

The two of them silently go through the lunch line, pick a few things, pay and then Dee follows Josh to a table along the right side of the dining room.

As they sit, Dee is the first to speak.

DEE

So you're new here too?

JOSH

Yea. We moved in July. My mom thought this school would be better for me, so we moved.

They pause for a moment.

JOSH

You just moved from Texas? Bet that was a move and a half. We just moved across town and I hated that.

DEE

It's not that bad. You do what you have to do, ya know?

JOSH

Yea, I know.

The conversation stayed fairly superficial until three rough looking boys slowly stepped up to their table. One of the three looks to be the leader. He speaks to Josh.

LEADER

Hey, Josh. Who's the girl?

JOSH

Hey Ron. This is Dee. She's new at school. I'm trying to be nice.

RON

I'll bet that's not all you're trying to do for her.

Josh looks up at Ron with an embarrassed frown.

JOSH

Drop it Ron.

RON

Do go Arnold on me man. Just messin' with ya.

JOSH

Right.

RON

We still on for tonight? It's your big night.

Josh hesitates a little and gives a quick half-look in Dee's direction.

JOSH

Yea, I'll be there.

                            RON

Bring your friend. She looks like it would be the
kind of thing that would light her up.

Before Josh could respond, Dee speaks up.

                            DEE

I'm free. What up?

                            RON

I knew it. I know my women.

                            DEE

I'm not one of your women.

                            RON

Whoa girl - back off.

All three pause for a brief moment.

                            RON

You want to come along, you can. You decide you
want to join us, we'll see what we see. Tonight's
tonight - let's leave it at that.

Ron and his two lieutenants start walking off.

                            RON

Nine o'clock. You know where to be.

Josh returns to his lunch without speaking. Dee presses him.

                            DEE

What's that about?

                            JOSH

You sure you want to know?

                    DEE

I did ask.

                    JOSH

Ron's the leader of a group here at Northside.
The Blades. They've been after me to join. They're
alright, but they get into some things I try to stay
away from.

                    DEE

Then don't go.

                    JOSH

It's not that easy. They made it clear that if I'm not
with them, then I'm against them.

                    DEE

They threatened you?

                    JOSH

No, no threats. I never pushed it.

The two sit silently for a moment.

                    DEE

So where do you and I meet?

                    JOSH

You may not want to be there. Tonight is my
initiation.

                    DEE

So what's that mean?

                    JOSH

I don't know. But I have to do it. I don't feel I have
a choice.

                              DEE

Count me in. It sounds like you may need a friend
there tonight.

Josh turned and looked into Dee's eyes. Her eyes were
quite beautiful and he seemed captivated by them for
a brief moment.

                              JOSH

I could come by and pick you up. Where do you
live?

                              DEE

Let's just meet. It's pretty far away. How about
meeting in front of the car customizing shop?

                              JOSH

You already know about Steve's?

                              DEE

Doesn't everybody whose anybody?

                              JOSH

I guess. Let's meet at Steve's. About 8:30?

                              DEE

I'll see ya then.

With that, Dee stands and takes her tray to the dish room
conveyor belt.

                                           CUT TO:

EXT. PARKING LOT IN FRONT OF A STOREFRONT CAR
CUSTOMIZATION STORE WITH THE NAME STEVE'S ON
THE FRONT IN NEON. IT'S JUST DARK. THE PARKING LOT
IS FILLED WITH HIGH SCHOOL AGE KIDS STANDING

AROUND IN SMALL GROUPS. THERE ARE SEVERAL
SPORTY LOOKING CARS IN THE LOT AS WELL.

DEE

Josh, over here.

JOSH

You made it. Are you sure about this?

DEE

I'll tell ya later after I find out what 'this' is.

JOSH

I know what ya mean.

They stand for a while by themselves talking about some
of the cars in the parking lot.

Ron comes up from behind them with about six guys with
him this time.

RON

So, you both showed up. Good. This should be fun.

JOSH

What's the plan?

RON

The plan is to make you a man.

Ron laughs and as he does his six laugh with him.

RON

That is unless your little girl has already takin' care
of that.

Ron and his six laugh again.

169

DEE

I'm no body's little girl Jerk

RON

I'd watch the mouth girl. I don't care whose friend you are. I'll torture you until you beg to be my little girl.

Before Dee could say another word.

JOSH

Leave her alone Ron. She's mine. You mess with her, you mess with me.

DEE (VO)

Wow, what a guy. He was defending me and we just met today.

Ron looked into Josh's eyes and pause for a long moment.

RON

Here's the deal. You do your thing tonight, and I'll stand by your rule about the girl. You drop the ball in my game though, and I get your stuff - all of it, and that includes the girl.

There was no reply. Ron moved on before anyone had a chance to respond.

RON

Let's get to it.

Ron walks off and the six follow him. Dee and Josh follow as well.

They all climb into a beat-up looking van that is sitting behind Steve's with the sliding side door open.

JOSH

I didn't know you had a van.

RON

I didn't until about an hour ago.

Ron's crew laughs except for Dee and Josh.

They vans starts and drives out of the parking lot.

INT. INSIDE THE VAN. IT'S AN EMPTY CARGO VAN WITH RON DRIVING AND EVERYBODY ELSE SITTING ON THE FLOOR THROUGH OUT THE VAN.

RON

Joey, give it to him.

One of the crew reaches into his jacket and pulls out a handgun. He hands it to Josh.

JOSH

What's this for?

RON

You don't expect the man to give you his money just 'cause you ask for it do you?

DEE (VO)

Ron's plan was becoming clear. Josh was to be part of a robbery. Probably a store of some kind.

As Dee is speaking above the action, the others pull handguns from their coats and show them to Josh. They ignore Dee.

RON

It was about to go down.

JOSH

What do I have to do?

RON

You don't have to do anything. If you want to be a part of my crew and protect your little girl, then you'll do what I tell you to do.

JOSH

OK, what?

RON

We're running short of pocket money, so we're going fishing. There's a spot on the south side that's ripe for the pickin'.

Ron drove on and all were silent. Dee and Josh were the only ones not smiling. The others were gleeful about their outing.

RON

There it is.

They slowly drive by a small liquor store.

RON

They should have our money ready for us about now. This is usually a busy night for them.

Ron pulls the van around through an alley behind the liquor store. He stops and leave the motor running.

RON

Joey, you stay with the van and keep it running. Mike, Pete, you two stay with him.

Joey nods and puts his gun away in his jacket.

RON

The rest of you are going in. You too Babe.

JOSH

No. She stays here.

RON

My crew - my rules. The girl goes, or you both are
out of my circle.

DEE

I'll be fine. I know my way around.

RON

I just bet you do. There's something very familiar
in your eyes. I think it what I see when I look in a
mirror at my own eyes. You've been around before.

DEE

I've been around. Do your thing and shut up.

RON

You heard the girl. Let's do it.

They each pulled winter sock caps over their faces as the
six of them step out of the van and walk down the short
alley to the front of the store.

INT. INSIDE THE LIQUOR STORE. SMALL, CRAMPED,
SHELVES PACKED FULL OF BOTTLES OF ALL SHAPES
AND SIZES. THERE ARE ONLY A FEW ISLES WITH THE
REGISTER COUNTER AT THE REAR OF THE STORE. RON
AND HIS CREW RUSH IN WITH RON GOING DOWN
THE CENTER ISLE AND THE OTHER SCATTERING TO
THE RIGHT AND LEFT AND ENDING UP AT THE BACK
OF THE STORE - GUNS OUT - ALL POINTING AT THE
CLERK.

The clerk in the store is an older man - about sixty. He is obviously shocked by the site of six armed hoods all pointing their guns at him.

> RON
>
> Give it up Pop. We want it all.

> CLERK
>
> Don't shoot. You can have the money, just don't shoot.

> RON
>
> You do your part and leave the rest to me old man.

Dee was staying next to Josh, watching what was going on. Josh was standing calm and still, but his eyes are pained as seen through the holes in the sock caps.

> RON
>
> That's good Pop. All of it.

He pauses.

> RON
>
> Hurry it up old man!

> DEE (VO)
>
> It sounded to me like Ron was working himself up to something. I think he wants more than money.

> CLERK
>
> That's all of it. All I have. Now leave and leave me alone.

Ron looks into the bag. It's obviously full of cash.

RON

Not so quick old man. We still have a thing or two
to take care of.

JOSH

Let's get out of here man. We've got the money,
let's go!

RON

Not yet pup. You still have to do your part.

JOSH

I've done my part. I'm here, right?

RON

No, no, no. That's not right. It's up to you to make
sure that we don't get identified later.

JOSH

Whataya talkin' about. We're all wearing masks.
He can't identify us.

At that moment, Ron pulls off his mask as his crew does
the same.

RON

Oh, no.

Ron speaks with a nervous playfulness.

RON

He's seen our faces.

JOSH

What are you doing? Let's get out of here!

RON

It's time for you to protect you leader. He's seen my face. If he talks, I go to jail and all of the rest of the crew as well.

CLERK

I'm not gonna talk kid. Just leave - leave.

Ron's voice takes on a mean, vicious, hurried tone.

RON

Don't kid me Pop. Now shut up!

DEE

Let's walk Josh.

RON

Keep your mouth shut girl.

Dee nearly growls.

DEE

You have no idea.

RON

Ouch, what ya gonna do girl? Bite me?

JOSH

Leave her out of this!

RON

Then finish it kid. Finish him.

Ron points his gun at the clerk.

JOSH

I'm outa here man.

Josh grabs Dee's arm.

JOSH

Let's go.

Ron shouts.

RON

No! Not that easy! You're here and this is gonna go down one way or the other.

A short pause of silence goes past.

RON

So, that's how it's gonna be. OK. I'll deal with it now and then I'll deal with it later.

Ron points his gun at the head of the clerk. Josh pulls off his own mask and moves at Ron with a quick sprint. Dee runs and stays at Josh's side.

JOSH

No Ron! No!

Ron turns the gun at Josh.

RON

Someone's gotta die tonight, it might as well be you.

DEE (VO)

I jumped between Ron and Josh as the gun went off. The bullet struck me in the chest. It was lucky I was wearing a loose jacket so no one could see that there was no blood coming from where the bullet hit.

JOSH

No! You Bastard!

Josh grabbed Dee's falling body before it hit the floor.

RON

Let's leave boys.

Ron and the others run off without hesitation.

With fear on his face, Josh gently lays Dee to the ground. He pauses for a moment,

Josh

I am so sorry Dee. I had no idea what was going to happen. I know it doesn't help, but I am done with Ron and his idiots. No more trouble for me, I promise you that. I wish I could help.

Josh stands, pauses as he looks at Dee, and then runs off the opposite direction from where Ron and his crew ran.

Dee is motionless on the alley concrete except for the movement of her mouth as she lay in the alley at death's door.

DEE

I can feel the last bit of life leaving my body. But how is this possible? I am created, not alive. I cannot die.

DEE

What is happening to me? I'm bleeding from the gun shot. How is that possible?

A dark, cold feeling moves through Dee. She has felt this before, many times. Satan was nearby.

The Boss

He walks slowly down the alley towards Dee. He is insulant as he berates her with his speech.

> So, I finally caught you cheating me. I knew from the moment that stupid little girl survived the fire you started that you were no longer on my team. She was so weak she should have died. But no! She ran from that building with the legs of an athlete, obviously healed by Him. But you had to set the circumstances in her favor or she would have still died — healed or not. Her parents would have divorced and lived in torturous pain for the rest of their lives. But instead, she lived, she was healed, they found new joy from the experience and will live happily ever after. What crap!

The Boss turns his back on Dee and begins slowly walking away. As he walks, he becomes less and less visible as if he is transferring back to his realm.

> So, after that, I decided that when I sent you on this assignment, I would make you human. You will die, and then all of the evil you have perpetrated will be laid upon you in my realm — under my terms. See you soon, Dispatcher; see you soon.

A small, peaceful smile comes to her face.

DEE
> I meant it when I said that I'd welcome death. Death is a far better option to following Satan's commands.

The smile leaves her face.

DEE

But still, I feel so sad.

She pauses, barely able to get these last words out of her mouth.

DEE

All the evil he will do - at least I was able to foil part of his plans ... for a little while. If only I could be forgiven...

EXT. A LIGHT STARTS GROWING FROM THE OPEN END OF THE ALLEY.

Dee's attention is caught be a growing light coming from above the end of the alley. She turns her head toward the light.

DEE

What's this?

A hint of fear crosses her face.

DEE

I see something moving towards me.

The look of fear passes and is replaced with a glint of excitement.

DEE

It's the blue-white light that I saw in the little Kelly's bedroom. It's hovering over me.

Dee smiles.

DEE

I feel so peaceful and unafraid. Is this death?

A deep, rich voice speaks from the glow.

DEEP, RICH VOICE

From this day on you will be known as Dee. Dispatcher is gone.

The light grows, saturating the alley.

DEEP, RICH VOICE

He knows your name. He knows all you have done. He knows that you choose not to be a slave to sin and torment. He knows that you choose to die rather than carry out any further hardship on mankind.

Dee responds smiling, but crying.

DEE

Yes, I would rather die.

DEEP, RICH VOICE

Anyone who dies for His namesake has been freed from sin. He died once for all of us. In the same way, count yourself dead to sin but alive to God, the Father.

The alley is now awash with the white light. All we see is white light while still hearing the Deep, Rich Voice speak with Dee.

DEEP, RICH VOICE

Sin shall not be you master because you are under God's grace for all of the good that you have done since the crucifixion. Your heart was touched on that day. You have been forgiven for all that went before.

Dee's sweet voice is heard.

DEE (VO)

At that very moment, I died. The very next moment, I was re-born to a new life.

Dee now stands in the same alley, in clear view as if it were a bright, sunny day, awash with white, wearing a flowing white gown with feathery wings spread wide and proud.

DEE

A new life as an Angel. Wow!

FADE OUT TO CRISP, PEARLIZED WHITE.

Printed in the United States
By Bookmasters